So This Was The Witch Who Had His Child . . .

She had the face of an angel . . . and the body of a seductress—which was a lethal combination for a man like him.

She was slim, and she moved with astonishing grace. Sunlight splashed over the vee of her neckline, and his gaze followed its path. Christopher felt so hot, he was burning.

He moved toward her and joined her in the dazzling fire of the sunlight. His hair fell across his brow, and he shook it out of his eyes.

She stepped back, aghast. "Why, you're not Gordon!"

"No." Christopher smiled. "You're not what I expected, either."

"Who are you?" she demanded in a low, amazed tone.

Her eyes met his, and it was as if she'd touched him. He saw the wildly fluttering pulse at the base of her throat, and he felt an answering excitement of his own.

She was the enemy, he reminded himself. *He liked her anyway. . . .*

Dear Reader,

Happy 1992, and welcome to Silhouette Desire! For those of you who are new readers, I must say I think you're starting the year off right—with wonderful romance. If you're a regular Desire fan, you already know what delicious stories are in store for you... this month *and* this year. I wish I could tell you the exciting things planned for you in 1992, but that would be giving all of my secrets away. But I will admit that it's going to be a great year.

As for January, what better way to kick off a new year of *Man of the Month* stories than with a sensuous, satisfying love story from Ann Major, *A Knight in Tarnished Armor*. And don't miss any of 1992's *Man of the Month* books, including stories written by Diana Palmer, Annette Broadrick, Dixie Browning, Sherryl Woods and Laura Leone—and that's just half of my lineup!

This month is completed with books by Barbara Boswell, Beverly Barton, Cathryn Clare, Jean Barrett and Toni Collins. They're all terrific; don't miss a single one.

And remember, don't hesitate to write and tell me what you think of the books. I'm always glad to receive reader feedback.

So go wild with Desire... until next month,

Lucia Macro
Senior Editor

ANN MAJOR

A KNIGHT IN TARNISHED ARMOR

SILHOUETTE Desire®

Published by Silhouette Books New York

America's Publisher of Contemporary Romance

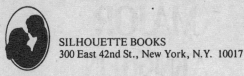

SILHOUETTE BOOKS
300 East 42nd St., New York, N.Y. 10017

A KNIGHT IN TARNISHED ARMOR

ISBN: 0-373-05690-7

First Silhouette Books printing January 1992

Printed in the U.S.A.

ANN MAJOR

is not only a successful author, she also manages a business and runs a busy household with three children. She lists traveling and playing the piano among her many interests—her favorite composer, quite naturally, is the romantic Chopin.

This story is for the young people who inspired it—
Lauren Major, Helen Brakebill, Kate Donaho,
Colin Guinn and Trey Guinn.

One

Christopher Stone jammed his foot on the brake pedal. Tires screamed and spun gravel as his Jaguar careened to a stop on the narrow private road of his ranch. Curls of dry summer dust swirled around the black car and obliterated his view of the desolate path that led up the hill to his beloved child's grave beneath a grove of trees—obliterated, as well, his view of the barren mountains and of his white ranch house perched atop a nearby hill that overlooked the dazzling Pacific.

From his notorious father, Christopher had inherited his golden, rebel-without-a-cause good looks. From his legendary mother, he'd received a restless, smoldering sensuality. His hair was reddish gold and rakishly long; his famous blue eyes were dark and stormy. He was well over six feet tall, with bronzed skin and the lean muscular physique of a man who spent much of his time out-of-doors.

The critics said he couldn't act his way out of a paper bag, but Christopher had an overwhelming screen presence. He was the highest paid actor in America. In his five *Tiger Force* movies, he had played the part of *The Tiger*, the ultrahero of the comic books and video games, who wore a mask and had a hidden identity. *The Tiger* was the adored idol of millions of little boys, but since Christopher never posed unmasked for publicity shots, he could go almost anywhere without being recognized.

Christopher ran his hand across the stubble of beard that he hadn't bothered to shave. He opened the car door and sank back against the seat when the dry desert heat engulfed him. The hills were wild and bare except for a few of his horses that grazed on the top of the hill. A pair of white horses stood apart from the others and turned their magnificent heads toward him.

He gazed at them without interest. Once, the ranch had been his favorite refuge from Hollywood and unwanted publicity, from his ex-wife, Marguerite, from all the demands of his film career and the hectic, fast-paced frenzy of his personal life. Now he hated the place. Maybe if he'd never moved out of L.A., Sally would still be alive.

Dear God. Today would have been her fourth birthday.

In his mind's eye, he saw her in happier days, toddling beside Marguerite's swimming pool in Malibu that was filled with huge brightly colored floats. Sally's favorites had been a green turtle and a purple dinosaur. The next vision was of her small body floating in the dark pool.

Christopher folded his arms across the steering wheel. He closed his eyes and he sagged forward as he rested his forehead upon his forearms. Pain spread through him like an innervating illness. His arms and legs were leaden weights. The tie at his throat was choking him. His suit was a straitjacket that made him feel sticky and hot.

He couldn't bear to walk up that lonely hill to her grave and read the letters of her name etched deeply in stone.

Why had everything he was, everything he owned, always meant so little? Why the hell couldn't he get on with his life and film *Tiger Force Six* like Cal wanted him to? Why did he continue to torture himself like this?

Because it was his fault. He should have known how to save her. Hadn't he, too, suffered the misfortune of having been born to Hollywood royalty? His parents had given him everything—fame, wealth, the best schools—everything except the things he most craved—their attention, love, care. Had he done any better as a parent?

From the passenger seat he picked up four red roses wrapped in cellophane and a battered stuffed horse that Sally had loved and had called White Horse, and he got out of the car. Slowly he climbed through the rocks and brown grasses until he came to her tombstone. He knelt in the shade before her grave. The four roses slipped through his fingers. He wanted to say something, but there was nothing to say. No one to hear.

Sally was gone. Lost to him forever.

He gazed up at the wide blue sky, at the blue ocean stretching endlessly. He was on top of the world, but all he could feel was the emptiness.

A twig snapped behind him and he jumped.

He could see no one in the trees, and yet he knew he was being watched by unfriendly eyes. He scanned the hills and saw only a faint breeze ruffling the brown grasses.

Then Marguerite's voice came from behind the largest tree, an ominous, disembodied whisper. "Very touching. Red roses and White Horse. *The Tiger* in a sentimental mood."

Hatred and loathing filled him. "What the hell are you doing here?"

"She was my child, too."

"When were you ever a proper mother?"

"You've got to be the most awful man God ever created!"

He laughed softly. "That should have made us perfect for each other."

Marguerite stepped from the shadows into the sunlight. She wore black with white pearls. Her wildly passionate, feline face with its high cheekbones and slanting eyes was carefully made up, her raven hair tied back in a black bow.

Her eyes burned into him with the hot dark force of a devil's eyes. He saw the sun glinting off the barrel of the gun she pointed straight at his heart. She had always been unstable, unpredictable. She could pull that trigger as easily as she might smoke her next cigarette.

The roses seemed vivid stains of blood on the brown earth. The bleak emptiness of the landscape was in his heart, in his soul. He was more dead than alive.

He stared at the gun and got up slowly.

If only she would.

He walked toward her, his bold blue eyes and insolent smirk daring her to do it.

"You're crazy!"

"Another virtue we share," he goaded.

"S-stop," she screamed.

When he didn't, her hands began to shake.

"Go ahead." His voice was hard and violent. "Put me out of my misery. You sure as hell put me in it. Finish me off the way you did our daughter."

Tears sprang into Marguerite's eyes. The gun wavered. Her fingertip trembled on the trigger. She hesitated, backed away from him, staggering clumsily, and then dropped the gun.

She sank to her knees. "You knew I couldn't."

"No, I didn't." The taunt in his low voice was like a spark set to dynamite. "Go ahead. Pick it up. Blow me away."

When she just stayed there, her face a turmoil of rage and despair, he leaned down to pick it up himself.

"You're always so smug, so ready to blame me for everything," she began. "It wasn't all my fault!"

"If it makes you happy to believe that—"

With an incoherent scream, she sprang at him. "You ruined my life, too!" She began pounding his chest, her long red nails clawing his face. "I loved her, too. I—I . . ."

She bent and twisted against him, but his arms were like iron. He crushed her hands behind her back and held them tightly until she broke off her struggles and burst into sobs.

He stared down at the wreck of her crumpled, tear-streaked face and saw through the blur of his own tumultuous emotions, a pathetic grief as profound as his own. They'd come as close as two people could to destroying each other.

He hated her.

How could he hate this poor broken creature?

He was amazed that he felt nothing, absolutely nothing. All his bitterness over their awful marriage and her part in the death of their child was gone. For the first time Marguerite's misery touched something deeper in him.

He had used her as a scapegoat so he could hide from his own guilt.

"I thought she was in bed that night," Marguerite said pleadingly.

He caught her in his arms and began to shake her so hard the black ribbon in her hair came loose and fell to the ground beside the roses. He didn't want to hear any of it. Her words brought back the horror of it all, and he drew a harsh breath. He wanted to lash out at her, to blame her as he always had in the past.

That was too easy.

"It was an accident," he managed roughly at last, letting her go. "There was nothing you could have done."

"You don't really believe that."

"Yes, I do. I know I've said and done things—terrible things—to you." He hesitated. "I'm sorry. Not that either of us can go back and undo any of it. Sally's gone. We won't ever have a second chance."

Inexplicably his words seemed to fill her with some new emotion. She started to say something, but no sound emerged from her trembling lips. Still, something in her desperation communicated itself to him.

"What's the matter?"

Her eyes widened, and she drew a deep breath.

Tears had made her rouge run. Gently he touched her cheek. Her hand came up and grabbed his, and for a long moment she clung to him.

"It wasn't your fault, Marguerite. I should have been there that night. I'm to blame for everything."

There was a look in her eyes he had never seen before.

"You don't understand," she whispered, her face twisting in an agony he couldn't fathom. "How could you?"

Then she turned and ran from him, stumbling down the hill.

Yanking the knot of his tie loose with one hand, Christopher sped along the freeway toward Malibu. What the hell could Marguerite want now? Hadn't they said it all last week at the ranch? The only thing he could think of was money. That's what everyone always wanted from him.

He drove fast, and with such impatient anger that he passed everything that moved. His air conditioning was blasting. His tape deck was blasting, too—hard rock music that pounded through him. Christopher picked up his car phone and restlessly punched in his agent's number.

"I'm sorry, but Mr. Fayazano is in a conference," Cal's secretary answered smoothly.

Nobody who was anybody in showbiz answered his own phone.

"Who may I say is calling, sir?"

"Christopher," he replied mechanically.

"Oh, Mr. Stone." The feminine voice became honeyed. "I can put you through immediately."

As usual, Cal came on the line with a roar. "Where the hell have you been? When the hell are you going to get back to me about *Tiger Six?*"

"I haven't read it." With one hand Christopher guided the Jaguar past a speeding Cadillac. The driver honked furiously.

"Work is the best way to forget your little girl."

Christopher heard Cal cover the mouthpiece and say to his secretary. "Tell him I'll call him right back."

Christopher stomped his foot down hard on the accelerator. A Volkswagen full of teenagers and surfboards pulled in front of the Jaguar just as the Jag leapt forward. Christopher had to brake suddenly. "Damn."

"What?"

Christopher's voice was brittle. "I don't want to forget Sally. You got that?"

"A year is a helluva long time for an actor..." Cal's gravelly tone died ominously. "Even a star like you, to stay out of the business. Younger guys pour into this town every day—leading-men types. Stars are short-lived commodities. You're not looking so hot, pal."

In spite of himself, Christopher shot a swift glance into the rearview mirror. He didn't much like what he saw. "So I had a bad night," he muttered.

"A year and a half of bad nights. Your fast life is showing, pal."

The three garage doors of Marguerite's sprawling pink palace came into view, and Christopher quickly pulled over two lanes, swerving in front of the Cadillac. He stopped in front of her triple-car garage. The Cadillac raced past him, horn blaring, a fist and finger elevated over the roof, but Christopher didn't notice. He was too caught up in the dark feelings of misery that the pink walls aroused in him.

Behind those walls he had lived with Sally and Marguerite until he had walked out.

"Bye, Cal."

"Wait a fungus minute."

Christopher slammed the phone down, got out and strode toward the wrought-iron gate. Rust dripped from the iron onto pink stucco. Dead bougainvillea vines clung to the trellises.

Marguerite damn sure wasn't keeping the house up, and it was his house, not hers. Marguerite had opted for cash in the divorce settlement. Then she'd become emotional and had refused to move. Christopher hadn't been able to boot her out when Sally was alive. Since Sally's death, he'd been too numb to care.

The intercom was still broken, so he jammed his fist hard on the doorbell and leaned against the wall.

No one came.

Damn. He rang it again and then kicked the wall; he picked a rock up and pitched it across the driveway. Then he went back to the wall, heaved himself upward, grabbing onto the top of it and yelling before he remembered the housekeeper spoke no English. He began again in fumbling Spanish just as the maid headed out the door to unlock the gate.

She didn't bother to look at him. *"Calmaté. Ahorita vengo."* Constancia was as short, fat and as sullen as ever.

He nodded and said sulkily, *"Buenos días,"* and dropped lightly to the ground.

She had never liked him. On the phone she always pretended she couldn't understand him. Today she corrected him. *"Tardes,"* she murmured under her breath.

"Whatever. Morning. Afternoon. What the hell difference does it make?"

She glared at him, pretending not to understand for a long moment. *"Nada,* to a man like you, señor." She turned and shuffled toward the house, and as he stared at the gate, he realized he was going to have to open it himself.

As he raced across unswept Saltillo tiles to catch her, pink stucco closed around him like prison walls. He saw weeds in the flower beds, filth in the fountains. Constancia led him across the patio into the house and shut the huge, hand-carved, wooden doors that Marguerite had scavenged in San Miguel de Allende from the ruins of a monastery.

Inside, Christopher felt close to panic. His throat was dry and choked. He yanked at the knot of his tie.

No lights were on. There was only the blinding glare from the ocean splashing across the large empty rooms. Only a perpetual gloom lingering in every corner.

Marguerite had sold the best pictures and the furniture. There were bare spots on the walls and indentations in the pink carpet. All that was left was the cheap stuff—a plush pink satin couch with armrests of tacky gold. And the mirrors. She hadn't gotten rid of those massive gilt-edged monstrosities she'd always loved preening in front of.

The worst thing about the house was the silence.

It had been a mistake coming here again. He went to a window, and that was a mistake, too.

Beyond the terraces and the swimming pool, the Pacific was blinding-white dazzle. All he saw was the empty heart-shaped pool. One night while Marguerite entertained a lover, his little girl had walked in her sleep out to that pool and drowned.

Today there were no floats. Only dead leaves drifted on that placid surface.

Dear God. He should never have agreed to leave Sally to film *Tiger Force Five* in Australia. The weekend she'd died would have been his weekend to have her, had he remained in L.A.

His throat burned as if a giant hand had squeezed his windpipe. He looked away.

Her voice caught him off guard.

"I didn't think you'd come."

He started.

Marguerite smiled. "You may go, Constancia." This in melodious Spanish.

Marguerite leaned against the golden arms of her hideous pink couch and made a false theatrical gesture for him to sit beside her. She called herself an actress, but like so many of the unemployed beauties in Hollywood who called themselves that, she almost never worked.

She wore a flowing purple dress that looked like a gypsy costume. Her black hair was bound by a purple turban. Immense gold earrings dangled to her neck. In one hand she held something that looked like a legal document.

Uneasily, he sat down beside her. "Why did you ask me to come by?"

Her rings flashed as she wrung her long slim fingers.

"Is it money—again?"

She flushed and then gave him one of her too-bright, theatrical smiles. "No...and yes."

He sensed a major problem. There was a long silence. He waited—restlessly crossing a leg over his knee and then uncrossing it.

"Christopher, I've done you the most terrible wrong."

He sprang to the edge of the couch. Like when had that ever bothered either of them before? She was very pale. Their truce since the ranch had them both off balance. If he couldn't insult her, what could he say?

She was staring uncertainly at the document. Carefully, she set it on a low, glass-topped table and smoothed it flat. "At the ranch you said we didn't have a second chance."

"Look, I don't hold you responsible." He couldn't stand being in the house with her another second. Poised to bolt, he stood up.

"No..." She touched his jacket sleeve. "You're always so impatient, Christopher. This is hard for me."

He sat down, took a deep controlled breath, and stared at the pink stucco ceiling.

"I should have done a lot of things differently," she said. "I—I cared about all the wrong things. I cared about you for the wrong reasons. I was even jealous of my own daughter because you loved her. Christopher, I've done you the most terrible wrong."

That again. He couldn't stand this.

"We both made mistakes," he said grimly. "There's no need to go into a maudlin recital of each and every one of them. It's not as if we can change anything."

"We can."

"What the hell are you driving at?"

She lifted the document from the table and handed it to him.

He snapped the crisp paper open and scanned it quickly. It was a birth certificate dated a year before their marriage. Even though the names of the mother and child were those of strangers, his heart began to hammer in quick, dull thuds.

He looked up again, puzzled, wary. "What does this have to do with me?"

Marguerite leaned toward him, her dark nervous eyes looking anywhere but at him. She brought a cigarette to her lips with trembling fingers and handed him her lighter. Dutifully he flicked the lighter open. Flame licked the tip of her cigarette. She sank into the pink cushions and inhaled deeply. "We had another child...another daughter...before Sally. Six years ago when I was living in Texas."

The dull thuds in his dry throat became a violent tempo. "You damn— Tell me you're lying."

She closed her eyes.

As he watched the smoke curl around her still-pale face, he knew she wasn't.

We had another child. In the tense silence of that shadow-filled room, the phrase repeated itself like a savage refrain in perfect time with the wild, palpitating rhythm of his heart. He clenched the paper, nearly ripping it until she gently pried it from his paralyzed fingers.

"Is she dead, too?" he managed at last, his whisper hoarse.

"No. She's alive."

Relief flooded through him. "Thank God."

"I used an assumed name at the hospital where she was born and made up a father's name. I told the lawyer and the adoptive parents that the birth father was dead."

"Wishful thinking, I'm sure."

"I couldn't have given her away if I hadn't. I thought you and I had broken up for good. You had gone to South America to shoot *Tiger Force Two*. I didn't know I was pregnant when you left."

The entire conversation seemed unreal. He wasn't really here in this nightmare house listening to this tale told by a madwoman.

"Why the hell didn't you tell me this before?" His voice sounded far away, like a stranger's.

"I tried to call you in South America, but you wouldn't take my calls. I truly believed you were gone for good. I grew desperate. I didn't want to raise a baby alone. When you finally came back, I'd already signed the final adoption papers. I was so ashamed I couldn't bring myself to tell you when everything was all right between us."

All right between us. His mouth thinned to a cynical line.

"I was so afraid I'd lose you again. I thought we would have other children, that I could forget that first baby. So I got pregnant with Sally quickly. But having Sally just brought the pain of my lost child back. I was jealous of you for being able to love Sally. I felt so guilty. I blamed you for everything."

In a daze he watched her squash out her cigarette and light another. So much came clear—her seeming indifference to Sally. Her depressions. Her irrational resentments and jealousy.

He buried his head in his hands.

Nothing they had done to each other mattered any more. Only this child.

A clawing surge of fresh paternal anguish threatened to tear his insides apart. Another child. Was she lost to him, too?

At last he looked up. Into the vacuous, slanting dark eyes of his ex-wife.

"Christopher, you have no idea what it was like to keep such a secret."

With an effort he managed to keep his voice level. "Why the hell are you telling me now?"

"Because it's haunted me." She smiled nervously in that bright artificial way of hers as she tapped her cigarette against the ashtray. "I should have told you a long time ago."

Watching that tapping cigarette, Christopher didn't trust himself to speak. She went on, easily. "I'm moving out of the house. I'm going on with my life."

"It's as simple as that then," he said.

"I can't help it if I'm not as complicated as you." She seemed to hesitate. "There will be certain expenses."

"So, it's back to money as usual?" A suave brutality laced his hard voice. "You've only been saving this juicy tidbit for the moment it would be worth the most."

She recoiled. "Why do you always have to be so nasty about everything?"

Dark animal emotion raced hotly through him. His eyes narrowed. He clenched his hands into fists. But when he spoke he kept his voice mild. "How much?"

She smiled. Studying him, she lifted her cigarette to her lips.

He stared at the slim beautiful face of the shallow, neurotic woman who had once held such captivating power over him, of the woman who had made him so unhappy for so many years. He was amazed to find that despite this new bombshell, he felt nothing for her. Even the hatred was gone.

Their passion had raged like a mutually destructive inferno until even the final hellish embers had burned themselves into extinction. In the cold void, it seemed incredible for him to imagine that he had ever been so deeply involved with her.

He was free at last.

Once he had longed for this moment—to be over her completely. But the price he had paid had been dear.

He pulled out his checkbook, and she named an appalling figure, which under any other circumstances, he would have told her was absurd.

He didn't flinch a muscle as he wrote the check.

It was nothing compared to all that he had paid before.

"Who has my daughter?" was his only question.

Two

What was Dallas, a highbrow scholar of metaphysical poets, doing in a run-down marina restaurant in South Texas, praying with more religious fervor than she'd ever imagined she possessed that her cook wasn't drunk again?

What bizarre twist of fate had left Dallas childless and manless for most of her thirty-two years and then made her the legal guardian of four, energetic hellions—*children* being a euphemism for this orphaned tribe of wild Indians? Guardian, too, of the failing restaurant and down-at-the-heels marina the kids had inherited, not to mention their pets—one dog, two molting parakeets, a blue heron, a much-abused gerbil, two aquariums and three cats?

It was Saturday night, and beach-weary customers poured into the marina restaurant. From the cash register Dallas Kirkland looked up expectantly every time the front door banged against the gray wooden wall.

Please, God, let it be Oscar. Please . . .

And every time it wasn't, her smile wavered. She kept hoping to see Oscar's craggy, weather-beaten face. She kept hoping to hear his surly growl of welcome as he swaggered past her in low-slung jeans carrying his jam box to the kitchen.

How gentle, cerebral Dallas would have longed for her old serene life at Rice University spent studying poetry, gathering research in hushed libraries and writing her dissertation—if she ever had a spare second for such longings. But there had been no spare seconds since her sister's death a year ago.

There was only constant chaos.

And disaster.

Unfortunately, tonight was a typical Saturday night. The restaurant was a tumbledown shack on pilings with big wooden decks sprawling over the Intercoastal Canal. The setting sun painted the warm waters of the canal livid red. The marina was a favorite stop for beach goers on their way back to the city from the barrier islands that fringed the Gulf of Mexico.

At the cash register Dallas played hostess, waitress and cashier. She frantically scribbled orders for shrimp baskets and burgers, took money and showed people to their tables. Through it all, she fought to keep smiling.

High above the register, a blue neon sign in the shape of the state of Texas flashed on and off. A muggy, salt-laden heat drifted through the open windows. Dallas loved Bach, but her customers, who drove trucks with huge tires and four-wheel drives, preferred the raucous Western music that whined from the jukebox.

Her thick glasses slid down the aquiline perfection of her perspiring nose for the hundredth time. She pushed them back, swiping at her wispy, golden bangs as well, and tallied the sum on her order pad.

"That'll be $32.56, please," she whispered, poking her pencil through the blond knot at the top of her head. She picked up a menu and fanned herself. The humid stir of air made her sleeveless cotton T-shirt stick to her damp breasts.

"What! $32.56?" her customer bellowed, slamming his half-finished beer down on the glass countertop.

When she nodded, the sunburned giant pushed his black baseball cap above his burn line and glared. She glanced past him at the line of customers. Slowly, his big red hands began counting out a wad of bills that looked as wet and bedraggled as he and his wife and kids did. He came up short.

"You got any money on you, honey?" he hollered to his wife whose plump cheeks were a perfect, sun-broiled match to his.

Dallas bit her lip as his wife set her beer down and fumbled through her purse. From a tangle of gum wrappers and keys, she plucked three torn dollars and two quarters.

Bravo.

Behind them, an impatient crush of customers curved around the back wall to the dark kitchen. More tires crunched outside on the shell drive. The front door kept banging.

Dear Lord. Dallas's tense gaze darted up to the clock under the blue neon sign. Where was Oscar? What was she going to do? It was madness to keep taking orders without him.

In the dining room and on the decks, the tables without setups outnumbered the tables with them. Instead of working, Rennie and Jennie, her twin teenage nieces, were fighting over the phone. Eleven-year-old Patrick had disappeared. As usual.

Kids!

The last strains of a Western ballad were dying as the customer handed Dallas his sandy clump of bills. As she made change, six-year-old Stephie tiptoed up to her, her dark innocent eyes flashing from beneath her black bangs with the immense self-importance of one who bears dreadful news.

With an anxious heart, Dallas sank to her knees.

"Oscar's laying on his couch, and he won't wake up. Not even after I pinched him. There's lots of bottles all lined up, and his breath stinks again, too."

Stephie's childish voice was faint, but Dallas heard every horrible syllable. Oscar was in his houseboat, drunk again, and Dallas wanted to cower under the counter for the rest of the night.

But the bill of a black baseball cap peeped over the counter. 'Ma'am, my change?'

"Stephie, go tell Rennie I need her. Run!"

Just as a sullen Rennie appeared, two silver-haired snowbirds barged to the front of the line. "We've been waiting half an hour."

"I'm sorry."

Dallas turned to Rennie. "Dear, you've got to cover the cash register."

"Aunt Dallas, I was talking to Jimmy Sparks!" A teenage moan of total despair. "And Jennie's talking to him now! What if he asks *her* out?"

"Concentrate on the cash register. I'm going to put Jennie in charge of the dining room and the deck."

"You'd better make Patrick do something, too," Jennie wailed as Dallas took the phone and said goodbye to Jimmy for her.

Dallas found Patrick, hiding out next door in the den of their house. He was curled in a suspiciously innocent pose, book in hand, in front of the TV. His favorite two cats, Harper and T.C., conspiratorially napped beside him on top of dozens of baseball cards.

"What were you watching, young man?"

Both cats' ears perked toward the sound of her voice. Patrick didn't bother to look up.

"Nothing." He spoke in a monotone.

She touched the top of the TV. It was warm.

She tapped it. "Patrick!"

His lips tightened; his cheeks reddened. That was his guilty look.

She moved toward him. Without looking at her he handed her the remote. She flicked it on.

The screen instantly filled with *The Tiger.* As always everything except the ultrahero's short blond hair and hard mouth was concealed, but his skin-tight costume revealed a male body that was lean and tough and sinewy.

Christopher Stone!

She was momentarily paralyzed.

From behind his black-and-gold mask, his bold blue eyes stared straight into hers. They seemed to touch her mouth and the swell of her breasts with such insolent contempt that she shivered. His jaw tightened. His dark male spell seemed to mesmerize her, and she gave a little incoherent gasp.

Was she crazy? He was a cartoon character. She despised the man as well as the role he played. With a shudder, she switched off the set. The very last person she wanted to think about was Christopher Stone. As if he hadn't made enough trouble.

He'd been calling her for days, making outrageous demands because, horror of horrors, Stephie was his biological child. He'd offered to pay all expenses that had been involved with her birth plus a lavish settlement toward her child care.

When Dallas had gone to her brother for help, Robert had sided with him, saying, "Mr. Stone is not our problem. He is the solution to our problem. You can have your nice life back at the university. We can send the kids away to the best private schools. And we can unload that dog of a marina."

"But that would mean breaking up the family. Stephie doesn't even know she was adopted."

"Then tell her. Sooner or later we all have to face reality, baby sister."

"Don't call me that."

"You're living in the real world now, not your ivory tower. And not on some fellowship or grant. The kids' insurance is almost gone. Soon, keeping you all will cost me a fortune."

"Not if I can make the restaurant and the marine pay."

"The miracle word is *if.*"

"You wondered why Carrie and Nick entrusted the kids to me and not to you. This is why, *big* brother."

Dallas hadn't spoken to her brother again.

The lamplight shone on Patrick's golden hair, and Dallas focused her attention on the boy once more. If only he wouldn't lie quite so often. "Your book's upside down," Dallas murmured quietly.

His flush deepened, and he flipped it over so quickly both cats jumped.

"Why don't you quit 'reading' for now, dear?" She picked up his book. "I need you out front."

"Things were different when Mother and Daddy were alive."

Dallas pushed her glasses up her perspiring nose and looked at him. "Don't I know it."

"They never made me work in the restaurant," Patrick continued resentfully. "You're not very good at running help or kids. Why don't you just give up like Uncle Robert wants?"

"Patrick."

"I bet you really want to take that money for Stephie so you can send the twins to boarding school and me to military school."

"Why, you've been eavesdropping."

"At least I know what's going on." With tearful eyes, he jumped up, jammed his hands into his jeans and stalked rebelliously past her toward the kitchen.

She longed to go to him, to pull him into her arms. But he wouldn't allow that except at bedtime. She set the remote on top of the television. "Patrick?" He turned. "I'm not giving up."

"Yes, you will." He opened the door, and she couldn't see his face. All she saw was the stiff, proud pose of his small body.

"I didn't quit the university and move in to take care of all of you because I wanted to send you to military school."

For a second he remained frozen at the door in his macho-guy stance. Then he was a little boy again, flying across the room into her arms. His cheeks were damp, but he made no sound. He always tried to act tough.

She knelt and clutched him fiercely. Until he finally insisted on pulling away.

"No one. Not even Mr. Stone is going to tear this family apart. I don't care if he does play *The Tiger*."

Patrick's voice was muffled. "*The Tiger* always wins."

"This is real life, honey."

"Maybe that's why I'm so scared."

Fires blazed beneath sauce pots. Oysters and shrimp sizzled in deep fat. Exhaust fans roared.

The marina kitchen was a madhouse, and Dallas in her white, grease-spattered apron was the madwoman at its center. At least, Pepper Canales, the marina's waitress, had finally come.

Dallas leaned over her cookbook and read. "Three minutes." Her glasses slid down her nose as she eyed a bubbly basket of pale, thickly battered shrimp that didn't look done.

Rennie came up to her and handed her the cordless phone. "It's Mr. Stone."

Not *again!* "I told you to tell him I was busy!"

"He won't take no for an answer."

Dallas grabbed the phone. "Mr. Stone, I won't sell Stephie to you and that's final."

"Did I ever once mention the words sell or buy where Stephie was concerned?" he murmured in a silken, holier-than-thou tone.

The muscles of her stomach constricted at the low, velvet-smooth sensuality in that maddeningly superior voice.

"Why do you always twist everything around to make me look like the bad guy?"

"Maybe because you are the bad guy, sweetheart."

"Good night, Mr. Stone." With a greasy finger she pressed a button and disconnected him. "There..."

Before she could hand the phone to Rennie, it rang again.

"You obviously want more money," the beautiful male voice whispered sweetly the second Dallas answered.

"You really are a loathsome man. I don't want your money."

"Those who have protested the loudest have always gotten the most," he replied cynically.

"Maybe you run with the wrong crowd."

He was silent. Then he took a new tack. "It's a pity you're not one of my fans."

"Mr. Stone, I despise the brutal, immature movies you make. You glamorize violence. You probably think you can take anything you want by force."

"If only I could," he purred. "So you *have* watched my movies?"

"Why don't you just hang up and leave me alone?"

"Because you have something I want."

Dallas was conscious of an implied intimacy in his words. His voice played with them, played with her. Blood pounded against her temples. She felt vulnerable, wary.

"I'm not one of your Hollywood starlets. Your fame, your money, your sex appeal will get you nowhere with me."

"I'm flattered that you think...I'm sexy."

Great clouds of steam rose from the pots on the stove. Dallas was so mad that she imagined invisible clouds spurting from her brain, as well.

"I can't deal with this—with you—at the moment," she whispered through gritted teeth.

"Maybe that's because you're not very good when it comes to dealing with realities."

She stared at the boiling pots, the sizzling fryers, the stacks of orders. "You don't know anything about me or the realities I have to deal with."

"Oh, but I do. Your brother has been a fount of the most fascinating information." Again, Christopher spoke with deadly softness.

"I can't believe that Robert dared to discuss me with you."

"He dared."

On a deep breath, she held the phone away from her face and glared at it. She felt furious and betrayed. And hurt. The tiny kitchen with its boiling pots and fryers was suffocatingly hot. She could see Pepper frantically darting about in the dining room, managing the kids and customers.

For a long moment the odious individual on the other end was silent, too. But in Dallas's imagination she could feel his fathomless blue eyes boring into her. She wanted to hang up, but she knew he would just call back.

What had Robert told him? Surely not... No, not even Robert would be that treacherous....

Still not speaking, she propped the phone against her ear and held it there with her shoulder. She began chipping a tomato onto four plates with quick savage strokes. When she was done, the vegetable looked like a madwoman had shredded it. A timer went off and she rushed to the oven and pulled out a tray of rolls.

Mr. Stone remained ominously silent.

Desperately, she checked her stack of orders and bent over the deep fat fryers. The shrimp wasn't ready yet.

At last Christopher spoke again. "Are you still there?"

"If I hung up, you'd just call back," she snapped.

"So we're beginning to understand each other."

"I wouldn't say that."

"But I would. Just what are you trying to prove with this Pretend-Mom-Cinderella routine? You didn't even adopt Stephie. Your sister did, and she and her husband died. Your brother told me you're the bookworm type."

"I'm Stephie's legal guardian."

"I'm her real father."

"I don't think there's anything *real* about you, Mr. Stone."

"Maybe you don't know me as well as you think you do." He started talking again in that deep sexy voice of his, only this time it was laced with bitter sarcasm.

Jennie dashed frantically into the kitchen.

"Just a minute, Mr. Stone." Dallas covered the phone.

"Aunt Dallas, Rennie and Patrick are making me do all the work again. Patrick took the garbage outside, and he hasn't come back. Rennie is talking to Jimmy."

"Why can't you kids ever cooperate?"

Rennie rushed in. "Aunt Dallas, table ten is getting mad."

"Tell them two minutes—max," Dallas whispered.

"Are you there?" Christopher demanded.

"Sorry. I'm afraid you're just one of the many crises I'm trying to deal with around here," she apologized in a sweetly false tone.

He uttered a low expletive.

"I find such language offensive, Mr. Stone."

"What exactly are you trying to prove, Miss Kirkland?"

Jennie grabbed two glasses of ice water and headed into the dining room.

A bit of grease splattered onto Dallas's arm.

"Ouch. Damn it."

"What happened?"

"As if you care." Instead of answering him, she drew a breath and sucked the wound until it stopped stinging.

"What the hell happened?"

"I burned myself. Okay? What am I trying to prove? Look, I'm just trying to hold a family together, a goal a man with your background couldn't possibly understand."

"Maybe I'm not some two-headed monster. I'm Stephie's father."

"Look, Mr. Stone, there's nothing fatherly about you. I've read all about you—about your famous parents with their ten marriages, about the custody battles they fought over you, about your little girl drowning in the swimming pool when you were a million miles away, about all your escapades since her death."

"I'm surprised a stuffy highbrow like yourself reads junk like that." His voice was cold and concise.

"It's hard to miss two-inch-high headlines when I'm in the grocery checkout lines. You don't know the first thing about being a responsible parent. The smartest thing your ex-wife ever did was give Stephie up for adoption so she could have a normal life. If I gave you Stephie, you'd destroy her."

There was a long silence. "How would you know?" he asked, his voice so hard and cold she shivered. "You never even had a kid of your own, Miss Kirkland."

The blood drained from her face. She clutched the phone more tightly. She closed her eyes and fought to ignore the pain. But that only gave him time to plunge the dagger deeper.

"Maybe you don't know much about raising kids yourself. Who made you God when it comes to deciding who should be a parent and who shouldn't?"

"The law," she said, frantic to be rid of this awful man. "I'm Stephie's legal guardian."

She scooped up a basket of shrimp and another of fries and tossed them blindly onto a platter.

"You'd still be the legal guardian to your blood nieces and nephew."

"Stephie is just as much a part of this family as they are."

"It's useless to argue with you," he said at last.

"I hope that means you're going to give up."

"Not on your life, lady." His last word was a careful insult.

"Look, I've got a dining room full of customers, shrimp to fry, mountains of potatoes to peel. My cook is drunk and didn't show."

"Sounds like the ideal environment for my daughter. Are you sure you can manage all that and care for a six-year-old, too?"

"Mr. Stone, goodbye."

"If we settle out of court, we'll all be better off. Stephie. Your brother—"

"Stay away from Robert."

"He's a lawyer, and he's on my side. He thinks it's in the best interests of all the children for you to give Stephie to me."

"My sister adopted Stephie. She entrusted her to me. I'd die before I'd let you have her."

"The last thing I want to do is hurt you, Miss Kirkland," he murmured in that velvet, tightly controlled voice. "I just want my child."

At just that moment a frightened-looking Stephie peered around the door.

How much had she heard?

Dallas sagged against the counter. "Dear Lord."

"What's the matter now?" Christopher demanded.

"It's Stephie," Dallas whispered. "She was listening."

Stephie raced into the kitchen and threw her arms around her aunt.

"Who are you talking to, Aunt Dallas?"

"Oh, nobody important, darling."

Christopher snarled some inaudible sound into Dallas's ear.

"What's adopted, Aunt Dallas?"

Dear Lord... Dallas was so upset, the phone slipped through her trembling fingers and splashed into the deep fat fryer. With a scream, Dallas grabbed Stephie and pulled her away from the stove and splattering grease.

Admidst curls of golden shrimp tails, one end of the phone bobbed out of the fryer like the stern of a submerged ship.

"Oh, dear..." Dallas murmured. "I guess that really is goodbye, Mr. Stone. The shrimp look done, too."

Stephie pulled at her apron. "What's adopted?"

Dallas forgot the phone and clasped the child more tightly. She looked into Stephie's huge, dark eyes.

"Oh, honey... It means... Your mommy and your daddy wanted you very badly. More than anything."

"But they're in heaven. Do you want me?"

Dallas felt a faint tremor go through Stephie's tiny hands. "You know I do."

"Does it mean I'm different than Rennie, Jennie and Patrick?"

"In a way. We'll have to talk about it tonight."

"Are you going to send me away?"

"Never. I'd sell my soul first."

Three

South Texas was bigger and flatter and hotter than Christopher remembered. It was uglier, too.

The only thing he liked about it was the endless blue sky with its dramatic thunderheads billowing against the horizon.

The sail across the bay from the city had been longer and choppier than he had planned. All he had on was a thin black cotton shirt and a pair of ragged white cutoffs. Even though his clothes were damp from salt spray, he was sweltering. His hat had blown off, so he'd gotten burned. He hadn't brought enough water, so he'd drunk way too many beers. As a result he felt slightly queasy—ill equipped to deal with the Kirkland witch, who had had the audacity to quit taking his calls after her lawyer had advised her not to talk to him.

His hand tightly gripped the tiller of his thirty-five-foot sloop. He was oversteering, but he couldn't seem to stop himself. He was used to board sailing, which was quite different from handling a yacht. From the canal he could see the marina. Heat waves made the restaurant, the decks, the house, the swimming pool and the docks shimmer. As he came closer he saw two kids on the dilapidated dock he was heading for. A dark-headed girl and a taller, blond boy who had a skateboard tucked under his thin brown arm were watching Christopher with the avid curiosity of experienced spectators who recognized impending disaster when they saw it.

Damn.

This was the first time Christopher had ever docked a yacht by himself. The last thing he wanted was an audience.

The film critics always said he couldn't act. He hoped to hell they were wrong because here he was in Texas about to play the most important role in his life. He usually wore his golden hair longer than he did in the movies. It was longer still, and he had dyed it a rich tobacco brown. He was wearing wire-rimmed glasses, too. Down below he had a duffel bag full of jeans, Western shirts and oversize belt buckles to give him the look of a Texas rancher.

As the white boat raced across the smooth water, he realized he was coming in way too fast. Only yesterday his sailing instructor had tried to warn him that he wasn't ready to sail alone. Nevertheless, here he was at the helm, recklessly giving it a try.

In his three sailing lessons. Christopher had always stopped by running into something. He ripped his glasses off so he could see. But the brown contact lenses he was wearing to disguise his famous blue eyes, muddied everything. He knelt to cut the power and jammed the engine into neutral.

Damn it. He was determined not to ram the dock this time. Still, as a precaution, he yelled, "Kids, you'd better get the hell out of my way!"

He might have done okay if he hadn't seen *her*.

The black-haired little girl was a six-year-old version of Sally.

His daughter.

She was barefoot and in shorts and standing a bit pigeon-toed just like Sally used to. She was holding a hermit crab. There was a blue heron beside her. Her long black hair was tangled as it blew about her face.

She was everything he'd imagined—soft, beautiful, adorable—and more. So much more.

And then she looked at him.

Until that moment he'd never believed in love at first sight. *His child. He had a living child.*

He knew a wild elation that was intensified because of the long months of grief, bitter guilt and despair. His gaze brushed the shining darkness of hers, and like a blind man who has regained his sight, suddenly his future held the promise of something very bright. He knew that no matter what it cost him, he would fight to win her.

He forgot the boat, the engine—everything save his child.

The white hull of his yacht charged toward her. The heron's great wings began to flap awkwardly. He saw Stephie's dark eyes fill with fear as she watched the huge bow wave. Her mouth gaped open, and she screamed. Then the older, blond boy yanked her hand, and they both raced for the safety of the shore.

Stephie's scream brought Christopher to his senses. He cut the power, shoved the tiller to starboard, jammed the gear into reverse, but he was too late. Although he missed the dock, the sleek white bow slammed into the concrete bulkhead, rode up it and then slid back into the slip on a shudder.

When a group of tourists drinking on the deck of the restaurant pointed at him and laughed, his cheeks grew even redder and hotter beneath his sunburn—if that was possible. He sheepishly ran his hand through his brown hair.

Not the inconspicuous landing he had hoped for.

But he'd sure as hell stopped.

The wind blew the yacht against the wooden dock.

His brain was still in a state of panic. What was he supposed to do next?

The boat started drifting out of the slip when he remembered—he had to tie her up. He lunged aft and grabbed a piling. He opened the lockers and pulled out a tangle of docklines.

The slim boy with his skateboard still tucked under his arm ventured back onto the wobbly dock. Stephie had run away.

It was just as well she had. Christopher was still so shaken from seeing her, he wouldn't have known what to say.

"Need any help, mister?"

"Nope." Christopher drawled the word like a native-born Texan. He was holding on to the piling with one hand and trying to untangle the line with the other.

The boy wouldn't leave. His young piping voice broke into Christopher's thoughts again. "Hey, you look sort of familiar."

Christopher started, but he didn't look up from the dockline. Hell, he didn't even recognize himself when he looked in the mirror. Then he remembered—his glasses. He'd taken them off. Quickly he put them back on and nonchalantly combed his forelock over his forehead. He looked up then and peered at the boy through his glasses, pretending they improved his vision. "Well, you don't look familiar," he drawled in his best Texas accent.

Now that the boat was no longer moving, the humid heat felt like one hundred and ten degrees. Christopher's black T-shirt soaked up the sun's rays and clung to his perspiring skin. He needed a cold drink, but when he opened his cooler there was nothing but empty beer cans floating in lukewarm water. He pulled out a can and crushed it with his bare hand before tossing it in disgust to the floor of the cockpit.

The kid watched him and then looked into the cooler. "Did you drink all of those—all by yourself?"

Christopher ignored Patrick and kicked the cooler over so that water and empty cans rushed out into the cockpit.

Patrick's eyes popped open. "No wonder you hit the dock."

"Damn it, kid."

"Patrick," the boy said in a level tone.

Christopher stared at him.

"Hey. Are you sure you couldn't use some help with those docklines, mister?"

Grumpily, Christopher tossed one onto the dock. Patrick threw his skateboard down and picked up the snarled line.

"You're pretty rough on your equipment, kid."

Patrick glanced from his skateboard to the black marks on the bow of the yacht. "Look who's talking."

Christopher's gaze narrowed, but so did Patrick's.

"You play hardball, kid."

They kept staring at one another for another long silent moment, two males challenging each other.

"I bet your mother's looking for you."

Patrick's stare wavered, and his hands fumbled with the knot, yanking at it harder. "I live with my aunt 'cause..."

For a second the boy looked like he might cry. But he didn't stop what he was doing, and the knot came loose. Deftly, he made a loop, slid it over a piling and tossed the end to Christopher.

Christopher remembered that the kid's parents were dead. Suddenly he was struck by something brave in this small, thin-faced boy. This kid tackled grief head-on and asked for no quarter.

"Hey, I'm sorry... Patrick." Christopher's drawl was deeper, gentler. Vaguely he was aware of a new respect as well as the flickering birth of some powerful emotion he'd never felt for any child other than his own.

Their eyes met again. Christopher's gaze was uneasy.

"It's okay," the boy said. A smile flashed fleetingly across his thin young face. "Really." He began to untangle another line. "Where're you from?"

Christopher shifted from one foot to the other. "I got a ranch, west of here." Which wasn't exactly a lie.

"You don't look like any rancher I ever saw."

Christopher grimaced.

Together they tied up the boat. Christopher was aware of Patrick going around after him and silently checking the cleats and retying most of what he had done.

After the boy had finished, and the boat was secure, Patrick lingered on the dock as if he didn't want to leave. "I could throw those cans away for you."

Christopher felt reluctant for him to go, too. "Okay."

Patrick bounded on board and began picking them up with the enthusiasm of a friendly puppy.

"Thanks," Christopher said.

"How long are you staying?" Patrick asked.

"Do you always go around sticking your nose in other people's business?" Christopher demanded. Only this time there was a trace of affection in Christopher's hard drawl.

Patrick assumed a tough stance and crossed his arms upon his skinny chest. "My aunt runs this place. I'm supposed to collect money from newcomers. I came down here to tell you not to take this slip 'cause it belongs to her boyfriend. And he's sailing over tonight. Only you took it before I could tell you."

"Then I'd better move."

"No!" Patrick glanced anxiously toward the damaged bow and the bulkhead. "I mean...I think you'd better stay right where you are."

Christopher remembered the way both kids had run for their lives, the way the heron had flapped for his, the way the yacht had plowed into concrete, and the memory triggered something he thought he'd buried along with Sally—

his sense of humor. Sheepishly he said, "No telling what I'd tear up getting out."

Patrick grinned from ear to ear. "No telling . . ."

Christopher smiled and reached across the cockpit and ruffled Patrick's blond hair.

For once, Patrick didn't pull away.

"Kid, you mind telling me something?" Christopher made his drawl sound very casual. He squinted hard at a billowing thunderhead. "How come you don't think I look like a rancher?"

"'Cause ranchers as old as you have faces and arms that are always real brown and leathery, and their foreheads and legs are real white—and they always wear jeans and hats."

"Well, er, that's how my men look. I stay inside mostly. I run things."

"Oh. Then you're not really a rancher?"

The kid couldn't have come much closer to hitting the nail square on its fibbing head.

Later, Patrick came back with papers for Christopher to fill out, a six-pack of canned drinks and two bags of ice. As Christopher watched the little boy swagger from the marina to the slip under the weight of the ice, he realized the kid reminded him of himself at that age. He hadn't been shy, either, and he'd always tried to act tough.

Christopher paid for a week. Patrick took his money and watched him write the phony name, Chance McCall, in a flourish of black swirling letters at the top of the page.

When the boy left, Christopher checked the nick in the bow. Then he got the hose and began to wash the decks.

Half an hour later, Christopher was still stowing his gear when he heard the purr of a diesel auxiliary. A beautiful yacht almost exactly like Christopher's was heading straight toward Christopher's slip.

Patrick ran out to the end of the dock beside the slip next to Christopher's and began waving his arms and shouting. "Over here. Take this one, Gordon."

Gordon glanced toward Christopher's yacht. A grim, pained expression marred Gordon's lean, tensely handsome face.

So this was Gordon. *Her* boyfriend. He was tall and thin with curly black hair. Christopher sipped his beer and broodingly watched Gordon land his yacht with perfect precision into the smaller slip.

There was an orderly way about everything Gordon did. He was wearing a floppy hat that tied under his chin, big dark glasses, a long-sleeved white shirt and long khaki slacks. Thus, Gordon was neither wet nor burned. He shifted into reverse, touched the tiller deftly, and the yacht came to a gentle stop dead center in the slip. Gordon picked up the correct lines with his boat hook and secured them quickly and efficiently with no help from Patrick.

Christopher watched as Gordon exchanged his sunglasses for regular glasses. He took out a leather case, cleaned both pairs of lenses, before putting one away and the other on. Then from an ice chest packed with ice that hadn't dared to melt, he took out an icy can of beer bearing a pricey foreign label.

Christopher got up and went over to introduce himself. "Sorry I took your slip."

"It was my fault he took it, Gordon," Patrick said.

"No, it was mine," Christopher cut in.

From the house a beautiful blond woman emerged and called to Patrick.

"I have to go," Patrick muttered, picking up his board and racing toward the house.

The two men were left alone.

"Gordon Powers." The stranger gave Christopher a long look before inviting him aboard.

"Chance McCall," Christopher drawled.

Where Christopher was tall and powerfully built, Gordon was even taller, although thinner, and more elegant. Gregorian chants were being played on the compact disc player down below.

"You're not from around here, are you?" Gordon said immediately.

"What makes you say that?"

"The accent. It's different."

Christopher flushed darkly. "I've got a ranch—west of here."

"Do you now?" Gordon gave him an odd look. "I'm an attorney." He held out a beer, but Christopher, who had had his fill of beer for the day, took a diet cola instead.

Gordon knew everything about every part of his yacht. Christopher wanted to question him about Dallas and Stephie, but once the guy got on the subject of his yacht's electronics, there was no diverting him. Gordon was smart, but listening to him was like hearing someone read an engine manual aloud in a monotone.

Christopher lay sprawled against a stack of blue boat cushions, watching Gordon twist black dials as he droned on about the technical marvels of each piece of equipment. The yacht had self-steering devices. Gordon could punch in numbers, and his boat would sail a perfect course for whatever mark he selected. It would tell him the speed and how long the trip would take.

"Hell, this yacht's a genius. No wonder you made a perfect landing," Christopher muttered at one point.

Gordon's eyes turned to ice. "The equipment was off."

That figured.

"Patrick tells me you date his aunt," Christopher prompted.

"Yeah, we've been dating for quite a while. Everything was great until she assumed custody of her nephews and nieces."

"You don't like kids?"

"I've got three of my own—and a matching set of ex-wives to go with them. I never see my own kids. All I do is pay. I was going to marry Dallas, but now—"

"Does she know how you feel?"

"She doesn't listen to me anymore. Dallas lets those kids run roughshod over her. She used to be a brilliant, sophisticated woman. But after only a year of living out here and dealing with four undisciplined kids, illiterate customers and drunk help, she's become totally irrational."

Christopher didn't find that hard to believe. "What makes you say that?"

"Well, one of the kids is adopted. The real father will pay through the nose for her. All Dallas has to do is give him his kid. We could farm the others out, and she could concentrate on me again. But do you think she'll listen—"

Christopher's hand tightened around his cola can.

Gordon was an ally. Why did Christopher have this insane urge to punch out the perfectionistic jerk's lights?

"Hell, no." Gordon's dark face grew grim. "She wants me to defend her case. Do you think she realizes that I can be choosy when it comes to women? They line up to date a lawyer."

They did more than that to get a movie star.

Later, Christopher wouldn't allow himself to dwell on what Powers had said because he found himself thinking of Dallas in a more sympathetic light—something he didn't want to do. What kind of woman turned down an easy life, sacrificed both her cherished intellectual interests and her own love life for the sake of four children who weren't even hers?

A bloodred sun was sinking into fiery waters when Patrick wandered, barefoot and shirtless with a fishing rod and a bait bucket onto the dock. Christopher went below. Without enthusiasm, he eyed the only food he had brought—a loaf of bread and jars of peanut butter and grape jelly.

He switched on a light and began reading *Tiger Force Six*. While his stomach growled, he scribbled notes in the margins.

The heat in the cabin grew stifling. His mind drifted from the script to Dallas Kirkland. Finally he poked his head out of the hatch. While Patrick fished, a great blue heron warily inspected the boy's bucket.

"Hey, Patrick, what's your aunt like?" Christopher asked.

Patrick's face softened. "She's neat! Nice! And as pretty as one of the angels in Stephie's book of Bible stories."

Sweet and pretty.

Damn. Christopher knew how to fight witches; he didn't have any experience with angels.

He needed to rethink this challenge. He decided to shower. He went back below, tossed his script into a drawer, switched the lights off in the cabin and went into the bathroom.

The shower was icy, but it felt good against his hot skin as it blasted away the salt and grit. Because of the running water, he didn't hear the melodious lilt of a woman's voice calling down to him. He dried off and then wrapped the damp towel around his waist and strode into the main cabin only to stop abruptly when he found a woman there.

She was framed in the hatchway, a vision of soft, female loveliness with the red fire of the setting sun backlighted in her golden hair and upon her golden skin.

She was peering into the darkness of the cabin. He was a shadowy presence she couldn't see all that well.

He recognized her instantly.

The highbrow. Stephie's guardian.

Only this woman didn't look much like a highbrow. Her thickly lashed blue eyes were luminous. There seemed to be tiny flecks of gold in them. Her fragile face was as perfectly sculpted as a porcelain figurine's.

She took his breath away, and he couldn't stop staring.

"Why, hello there," he whispered.

She was beautiful, but not in the way he was used to. He knew she was no young virgin, but she looked like one. Her education—obviously mainly from books—had not touched her in the way that his real-life experiences had hardened him.

"Surprise, darling," she said softly, welcoming him with a sweet warmth he had longed for all his life.

Gordon Powers was a lucky bastard.

Christopher's heart pounded. The teak flooring seemed to rock gently beneath his bare feet. He sensed some new, never-known-before danger. Against his will, he was drawn to her.

"I cooked you some shrimp—your favorite."

Then it came to him; she couldn't see him in the darkness. *She thought he was Gordon because he had taken Gordon's slip.*

Christopher knew he should tell her who he was at once, but he didn't want her to go. Not yet.

She was the enemy.

The unusual gold flecks in her irises caught the light of the sun and sparkled.

But a beautiful enemy.

He had always had a weakness for beauty.

"Shrimp. How nice of you," he murmured.

"Sorry I was late," she said. "I wanted to cook the kids a balanced meal and get them settled for the night so that we..." Her voice died on a suggestive note.

"That sounds too good to be true," he whispered hoarsely. "Wonderful."

"I've been neglecting you," came that velvet, heart-stirring voice.

"Is that a fact?" he asked enthusiastically.

"But all that's going to change—tonight."

"I can't wait."

She began descending the stairs. His hungry male gaze followed her thin, elegant, bare feet and ankles, her long golden legs, the swell of creamy thighs. She was wearing skin-tight white shorts and a thin T-shirt that molded her body. His throat felt hot, dry.

So this was the witch who had his child.

Patrick was right. She had the face of an angel.

And the body of a seductress.

Which was a lethal combination for a man like him.

She was slim, and she moved with astonishing grace. Sunlight splashed over the vee of her neckline, and his gaze followed its path. Christopher felt so warm, he was burning.

He moved toward her and joined her in the dazzling fire of the sunlight. His hair fell across his brow, and he shook it out of his eyes.

She stepped back, aghast. "Why, you're not Gordon!"

"No." Christopher smiled. "You're not what I expected, either."

"You should have told me who you were at once," she said.

"Indeed?" His lips parted into one of his quick, bold smiles. His eyes went over her and flashed just as boldly. "I've never been able to resist...anything so delectable looking..." His gaze lingered over her breasts, her narrow waist, her flaring hips. "So absolutely delicious in appearance..." His ravenous gaze finally settled on the shrimp. "As home-cooked...crustaceans."

She blushed charmingly from her sun-kissed nose to her neckline, and he moved closer to pluck a shrimp from her trembling hands.

Their fingers touched, and a swift hot current raced through them both.

She jumped back, startled.

He told himself it was just his sunburn that made his skin tingle. He took a shrimp from the platter. It was still sizzling, and it burned his fingers. He popped it into his mouth. His white teeth crunched into it. Then he swallowed it. His hot gaze roamed her lush soft curves. "Delicious." He grinned broadly. "You're a very talented ... lady."

"Who are you?" she demanded in a low amazed voice.

"Your guest," he murmured. He bit into his second shrimp and quickly ate it. There was something very sensual about eating shrimp and watching her. He licked his lips. "I didn't realize I was so ... hungry."

Her frightened eyes met his, and it was as if she touched him. He felt on fire. He saw the wildly fluttering pulse at the base of her throat, and he felt an answering excitement of his own.

He was used to women wanting him—because of who he was. But this was different.

She was the enemy, he reminded himself.

He liked her anyway.

"Don't be afraid," he said. "Not of me."

"Oh, I'm not."

He heard the husky quiver in her voice.

"Oh, yes, you are."

Shakily she moved a tendril of golden hair out of her eyes.

He kept staring at her. She was more beautiful in person than she had been in the pictures his private detective had furnished him with. He was used to photogenic women, to being disappointed when he actually met famous film beauties.

She clutched the railing by the stairs.

Vaguely, he remembered his glasses—who he was, who he was supposed to be—and the danger to his plan if she recognized him. Fumbling, he grabbed his glasses from a nearby shelf.

"I wish I was wearing mine," she said weakly as she watched him put them on. She was making the kind of inane conversation strangers make to avoid an awkward silence.

"What?"

"My glasses. Gordon prefers me in my contacts."

"Gordon?"

"I thought this was his boat." She kept playing with that golden tendril, winding it and unwinding it around a fingertip.

"Oh, yeah. Powers. I...forgot all about him. I met him. I sort of accidentally took his slip."

"Your boat is almost exactly like his. I'm sorry to have bothered..."

Christopher moved nearer. "Sooner or later we were bound to meet."

She sank against the stairs, but she was so close he felt her breath, light and warm, flutter against his throat. Her sweet fragrance enveloped him. He felt hotter than ever.

"Maybe it's divine intervention," he said smoothly.

Her fascinated gaze ran fearfully over his muscular arms and chest, stopping where his hard brown abdomen met the stark whiteness of terry cloth. Her flushed look made every cell in his body conscious of his male nakedness beneath the towel.

"I—I don't think so," she whispered. "I made a mistake. Not that I blame you for getting the wrong impression."

"Are you sure it is a *wrong* impression?" he queried softly.

"I'm not that kind of girl."

"What kind?"

"The kind you think I am."

"So you can read my mind?" His eyes gleamed.

Her senses seemed to catapult in alarm. "I'd better go."

He laughed, a husky throaty laugh. "You just got here."

"But I don't know you."

His sensual mouth curved. "Then I'd better introduce myself."

"No!"

Again he laughed.

"Please..."

His gaze lingered on her golden throat. He watched the wild beating of her frantic pulse at its base. He saw the faint beading of delicate perspiration drops there. More than anything he wanted to reach out and touch her. Would her skin feel like satin? Would her mouth be delicious?

He *had* to know.

He thought she read his every thought. The pupils of her eyes grew so enormous that only a ring of blue encircled them.

"I'm not going to hurt you," he heard himself say.

Slowly his hand touched the curve of her shoulder, moved up her throat to her earlobe. Gently he stroked her.

She was soft, warm, living satin. She didn't move away from him. Instead, she sighed deeply on a long shudder.

He felt the heat of her engulf him, and his own breathing grew harsh. His lips longed to follow the path traced by his exploring fingertips. He lowered his dark head toward hers, and she began to tremble.

The world grew very still.

"No," she whispered, frantic.

She was quivering like a frightened animal, wanting him to kiss her and yet terrified. There was some mysterious duality in her nature. She was hot, eager. At the same time she was as cold as ice. He sensed that to kiss her now was to lose her forever.

So he stopped.

For a long tremulous moment she stayed there, powerless to move her body or her eyes away from his.

He stepped back to give her breathing room, and that was a mistake. She flew up the stairs. Christopher forgot he was wearing only a towel and raced after her, stopping short when he saw Gordon standing on the dock.

Gordon's expression darkened as his gaze swept from his girlfriend to the beaming, towel-clad Christopher.

"What the hell were you doing down there with him?"

Dallas was too upset to answer.

"Don't ask," Christopher murmured on a suggestive note.

Gordon grew even angrier. "You stay out of this!"

"Just trying to be helpful," Christopher said cheerily.

"Oh, dear...." Dallas wailed as she clambered off the boat.

"The last thing I want to intrude upon is a lover's quarrel," Christopher said, his manner meek and overly solicitous.

"We are not lovers!" Dallas screamed down at him.

Christopher felt sharp joy at that declaration, but he made his face carefully grave. "Sorry. Wrong impressions...again."

As he descended the stairs that led to his cabin, he didn't look the least bit sorry.

"You started this!" Dallas shouted down to him.

He paused on the stairs. "Thanks for the shrimp."

"You gave him my shrimp?" Gordon's voice thundered. To Christopher he yelled, "Give them back, you fiend."

Christopher looked at Dallas. "Fiend? Maybe if he had asked me nicely—"

"I said fiend and I meant fiend!"

Christopher snapped his hatch shut as Gordon howled with rage. Christopher's windows were open, and he heard their muffled voices.

"I thought he was you, Gordon."

"The hell—"

"I really did. I mean... Oh, it's too confusing to try to explain."

Christopher heard Gordon explode. "Get them back!"

"What?"

"My shrimp!"

"You mean, go back down there?" She was aghast. "What if he takes his towel off? Besides, he's probably already eaten them."

She knew him better than she imagined.

As she spoke, Christopher ripped off his towel and plunked another shrimp into his mouth. It was moist, succulent—delicious and a hell of a lot better than peanut butter.

He pulled his script from his drawer and reached for two more shrimp.

Enemy or no, she was damned talented in the kitchen.

He remembered how hot and silken she'd felt in his arms, how she'd jumped back when he'd touched her, and he wondered about her other talents.

What would she be like in the bedroom?

Four

What would she be like in the bedroom?

As Christopher sat alone in his darkening cabin, contemplating this question instead of the script that kept blurring, a dozen male fantasies came and went in his overly active imagination.

In his favorite, Dallas lay naked across his forepeak bunk with her golden hair tumbling about her soft body. The golden flecks in her brilliant eyes were wantonly ablaze as this delectable phantom enticed him to her by crooking a fingertip.

On a groan that was half angry frustration and half jealousy, Christopher threw his script down. He rubbed his eyes with the back of his hands.

Dear God. What was he doing to himself?

The tiny windows didn't let in any breeze, and the cabin was stifling again. He arose and slid open a hatch.

The purple sky was blackening. The humid air smelled as tangy as the marshes. On the distant horizon, the city's lights twinkled like diamonds, but the beauty of the night was lost on Christopher. All he could think of was her.

Banjo music drifted from the restaurant as did sounds of boisterous laughter. Although he was hungry, he wasn't tempted to join the raucous festivities. He was too conscious of the yacht next to his, too conscious that Dallas had gone below with Gordon and stayed there—alone, with him, for hours. He kept seeing her as he'd imagined her in his cabin. Dear God. Christopher kept remembering the way she'd looked so soft and lovely with the fire of the sun in her golden hair. She'd been so anxious to get away from him.

What the hell was she doing down there so long with Gordon?

The Gregorian chants were still playing—the Credo, the Agnus Dei. What kind of guy played weird stuff like that when he made love to a woman? Maybe highbrows who read John Donne and Andrew Marvell liked religious chants. She damn sure hadn't come out of *that* cabin.

Who was running the restaurant? Who the hell was taking care of Stephie? Christopher remembered all the arguments he'd had with Dallas over the phone when she'd thrown up the sensational stories about him as proof he was too irresponsible to care for his child. He stared at Powers's yacht. Who was *she*—to call him irresponsible?

Above the chants, her whisper floated to him. "He's out there—watching us. I can see him."

"Relax. Forget him."

A light flicked on in Gordon's cabin.

"I—I can't," she said. "He's just sitting there. Maybe if he'd go below..."

"What do you want me to do—go ask him?"

"No!" She sounded frantic.

Christopher turned on his own radio to a rock station. The hard beat obliterated the softer psalm tones.

A second light flicked on in their cabin.

Christopher turned up the volume of his music. He felt like he was involved in a bizarre duel for this woman, his enemy. Through the portholes, he could see the man and the woman clearly. They were seated on opposite bunks, arguing now.

For the first time he noted how reflections from city lights and the sparkling stars turned the dark water to shimmering satin. He gave a low whistle as he appreciated what a hell of a pretty night it was—even if it was Texas.

It grew later, the night blacker, the stars brighter. Christopher's loud rock music was the only music still playing.

The childish sob that woke him was soft and fragile.

Christopher shot bolt upright.

A little girl was lost and crying somewhere in the night. *Sally.*

In a thousand dreams he'd heard her soft cry.

But this wasn't Sally.

The soft frightened cry came again.

He wasn't dreaming.

He heard the metallic clanking of the shrouds against the mast, the lapping of the water against the hull. The thick heat enveloped him. His body was bathed in perspiration.

He was in Texas.

The terrified whimper came again, and a cold caress of fear raced down the back of his neck.

He jumped up and snapped on his jeans. Deftly he turned the music down. When he came out of his cabin, the yacht next to his was dark and silent. So was the restaurant. There was no moon; he couldn't see anything but stars and the distant city lights. The wind had died to a breath.

He heard the broken sobs again, and he sprang lithely onto the dock. A white nightgown fluttered at the far end of the dock. A little girl with long black braids was walking across the rough wooden planks.

Stephie!

His daughter!

He started to call to her and stopped himself.

As a child he'd walked in his sleep. So had Sally. He remembered how terrifying it had been to be awakened suddenly and to find himself in a strange place with a strange person.

"Stop," he whispered. "Please. Stop."

As soundlessly as a ghost, she glided toward the deep black water at the end of the dock.

"Stephie . . ."

Black braids twirled. The lacy hem of her nightgown tangled around her legs. Her glazed eyes stared through him unseeingly. "Mother—"

"No, honey. I'm your—" he choked on the word "—father."

She gave a terrified little cry and ran.

This was worse than his recurring nightmare. In his dreams, Sally was crying, and he was an impotent statue, unable to do anything other than stand by helplessly and watch in horror as she sank into the pool.

Not this time. This wasn't a dream. This was Stephie. He was going to save her.

When he sprinted across the rough slippery boards, a protruding nail tore his heel open. She took a faltering step; her tiny foot found empty air. She cried out, but he was there behind her. As she fell, he caught her.

His child.

He knew an intense paternal thrill as he lifted her firm little body to safety. What he wanted more than anything was to take her away with him, but the minute he seized her, she came awake wildly. She opened her eyes and read the deep emotion in his. Her wiry body began to writhe. She was little, but she kicked like a mule.

"Easy," he whispered gently.

She pressed her hands against his chest and screamed. "Aunt Dallas!"

"Honey…honey…." In vain he tried to soothe her as he carried her onto his boat. In his cabin he found Sally's stuffed White Horse.

Stephie threw it overboard and screamed more loudly.

His torn heel left a slippery trail of blood across the white decks of his boat as he lifted her back onto the dock.

Out of the darkness Dallas came flying. With the starlight in her hair, she seemed an ethereal girl running lightly toward him. She was still wearing the same T-shirt and white shorts she'd worn earlier, but her pale face was stricken with fear when she saw him with the child.

"Let her go," Dallas commanded.

"I wasn't going to hurt her."

Dallas's eyes flashed coldly. "Let her go." Like Stephie, Dallas saw him as a threat instead of as a savior.

"I swear I wasn't—" He broke off. It was useless to argue when he was already tried and condemned. Very gently, he knelt to the dock and released Stephie.

"Stephie, darling." Dallas's voice was velvet soft.

Stephie ran eagerly into her aunt's arms. Dallas cradled the child against her breast. At first he felt awkward and rejected as he watched them. Then despite Dallas's coldness toward him, he felt drawn to her. She knew just what to say and do to soothe, just how to answer each of the child's frantic questions. Marguerite had always been too impatient to comfort Sally. His own glamorous mother had never comforted him.

Then he remembered the long hours Dallas had spent with Gordon. Had she been with him still when Stephie had walked in her sleep? Marguerite had been with a man the night Sally had drowned. The horror of Sally's death came back to him and with it, all the old hatred. He zeroed in on Dallas.

His deep voice sliced through the darkness. "Where were you tonight? Why weren't you looking after her?"

Dallas looked up, startled. He towered over her. Still holding the child, Dallas stood up. "I was looking after her, but she walks in her sleep sometimes."

"Tell me about it. If I hadn't heard her, she would have drowned." His face was grim. "You were with Powers."

"That was hours ago."

Christopher glowered accusingly down at her.

Dallas's thickly fringed lashed lowered. "Just who do you think you are?"

Stephie quit crying and attacked him, too. "He grabbed me!" The little girl studied him with huge suspicious eyes. "He was going to kidnap me!"

Stunned, Christopher looked down at his daughter. So, that was why she'd been so scared. She'd intuitively sensed his true feelings. Not that he would admit anything.

"The hell I was! I grabbed you because you were about to walk off the pier!"

"You were too taking me away!" Stephie began to weep dramatically again.

Before he could defend himself, Dallas leaned down and touched his foot and then the smear of blood on the dock. Her gentle touch warmed him through.

"No, darling." She rose slowly. "I—I believe him. He did save your life. And he hurt himself."

Stephie eyed his sharply etched face, his foot, and the bright blood on her aunt's fingertip with grave doubt.

"You should say thank you to the nice man."

"He isn't nice, and I won't say it."

"Then I'll have to say it for both of us." Dallas lifted her lovely face framed with trailing golden hair and stared directly into his eyes. "Thank you," she said softly.

His gaze devoured the delicate curve of her lips. Why couldn't he forget that her skin had felt like molten satin that once? Why did he crave to touch her?

"You're welcome," he replied curtly.

They stood there staring at each other.

"Well—" she broke off nervously.

He laughed just as nervously. She turned to go. But when she carried Stephie toward the house, he followed them.

There was another awkward moment when Dallas discovered him behind her on the porch. She sighed deeply, not knowing how to deal with him. "Thank you...again."

She meant goodbye. But when she pushed open the screen door, he held it for her and then boldly followed them inside to the kitchen.

She looked surprised at that and stared again, but before she could react, a blond teenager with the name Rennie painted across her T-shirt bounded down the stairs. On the third step she tripped on a skateboard and fell.

Unfazed, she pulled herself up. "You found Stephie!"

Dallas tugged a loose red ribbon from Stephie's braid and set it down. "She walked out to the dock. If it hadn't been for—" Dallas turned uncertainly toward Christopher, caught an eyeful of gleaming male torso and blushed.

Suddenly he felt tense and hot and embarrassed without his shirt. His brilliant gaze touched her mouth, the rounded curves of her breasts before he forced himself to look away. When his glance settled on the chrome toaster, damn it if his face wasn't as red as hers.

After that look, neither adult heard a word Rennie said. They were both fighting a losing battle to ignore each other.

"You little rascal!" Rennie said, breaking the tension. "All the way out to the dock! That water's so deep."

"Yes," Dallas said. "But the danger's passed now. Rennie, dear, would you please take her up to bed?"

Stephie defiantly buried her face against her aunt's neck and clung.

Dallas pleaded gently. "Darling, I'll be right up."

Stephie held on.

"Please, dear, so I can tell the nice man who saved you goodbye."

Stephie turned big wet eyes on him. "He isn't nice."

"Stephie, you're being rude."

"What if he's my birth daddy—come to take me away?"

Dallas went as white as paper.

Christopher felt as if he'd been punched in the gut. *Was it all over—so soon?* He stiffened.

Dallas was the first to recover. "So, that's why you were so scared." In her gentlest tone she began, "Darling, he isn't, and even if he was, didn't I tell you I wouldn't let anyone ever take you away?"

Christopher sucked in a long tight breath.

"Now, run along upstairs with your sister," Dallas said.

From the stairs Stephie cast one last dubious glance toward Christopher before racing up them. Then Dallas and Christopher were alone in that homey kitchen littered with kids' sneakers, dishes, bait buckets and cans of pet food.

Their glances met. Never had he been more aware of a woman.

Hastily she averted her gaze and picked up a pair of dirty socks and shakily stuffed them into some tennis shoes. "Have you eaten?"

Christopher cleared his throat. He shook his head.

"There's a bathroom right through that hall where you'll find Band-Aids and medicine for your foot."

While he was tending to his foot, Dallas prepared something to eat. When he returned, she set a plate of warmed-over fried chicken and beans before him and sat across from him. "We can talk while you eat."

But they didn't talk, and Stephie's comment about him being her birth father stayed in Christopher's mind. The kid was smart, and she was on to him.

"Your chicken was even better than your shrimp," he drawled in a low tone, on guard.

She set her coffee cup down. "Chicken used to be my specialty."

He'd felt awkward eating, but he felt more awkward now that he was through, because he couldn't be honest. He tried not to look at her, but every time he did, he felt himself react. Her golden hair circled her face like a halo. Every part of her seemed delicately made and enticingly feminine. For some reason he couldn't think of a thing to say—which was odd. He was used to beautiful women. They had always been easy for him. Why wasn't this one?

"The food was great, really great." He caught himself. "I already said that, didn't I?"

She sat across from him twisting her fingers.

"You didn't need to feed me," he went on.

"It was the one thing I could do—to thank you." Her voice was soft.

"Hey, there was no need."

She was so sincere. He felt like a heel.

Dallas touched his hand, and her velvet warmth flowed into him. Then she looked at her fingers there and she blushed. As quickly as she had touched him, the hand fluttered back to her lap.

He gazed into her frightened eyes. There were mysteries attached to this woman. She didn't trust him. Was it just him? Or all men? He needed to go slowly, very slowly. That wasn't his style.

"Maybe I shouldn't have eaten Gordon's shrimp this afternoon," Christopher conceded in a halfhearted apology.

"Gordon was pretty upset." Her smile was dazzling. "He's possessive. What's his is his. You may not understand that sort of thing."

Christopher picked up Stephie's red ribbon. His roughened brown fingers tensed around the soft satin. Deliberately, he set the ribbon back down. "Oh, I understand." A pause. "I know I haven't any right to ask this." His hard eyes met hers. "Do you belong to Gordon?"

"I—I don't belong to anyone." She was very pale.

"What a shame. You're a beautiful woman."

Paler still, she drew back. "It's the way I want it."

"You're sure?"

"Of course." Her uncertain gaze darted everywhere, but to him. Her voice was very faint. Now she was the one fidgeting with Stephie's red ribbon. "Why did you come here anyway? You're not like anybody I ever met before."

"You make it sound like a sin."

"Maybe that's because it feels like one."

"Is that good?" he murmured. "Or bad."

Her eyes filled with wild emotion. "Just dangerous." Her words died away and left a tension-filled void in the quiet of the kitchen.

"That spells good in my book," he replied, his voice like silk as he watched her lick her dry lips.

She was the one woman he shouldn't even think of, yet he was fiercely conscious of her. He felt excited, restless, wanting something from her that was utterly different from what he usually wanted from a woman.

He leaned closer. For an instant, a charged silence seemed to hang between them. Then she got up so fast that her chair crashed against the linoleum. The screen door banged as she ran outside onto the porch, away from him.

She was scared now. What would she be like when she found out who he really was? Thoughtfully he picked her chair up and set it against the table. Then he pushed the door open. She was leaning against the house, hiding in the shadows, hugging herself. The faint breeze made the bronze wind chimes tinkle. His pulse quickened as he drank in the sight of her.

"What are you trying to do?" she whispered across the darkness.

He stepped outside. "I don't know myself half the time."

"I belong to myself," she murmured in a ragged voice.

"If that's the way you want it."

"That's the way it has to be."

The moonlight turned her hair to silver.

"Really?" He moved nearer. "Why?"

Her breath caught in her throat. "You've got to go now." She shrank against the house. "Back to your boat. I want you to sail away from here and never come back."

"Do you now?" He was standing so close to her, he felt the enveloping warmth of her body. He inhaled the delicate scent of her. "Honey, it's not going to be that easy—for either of us."

Reaching out, he seized her shoulders. A thrill coursed through him even as he pulled her, trembling to him.

"Easy, honey, I'm not going to hurt you."

"Maybe you won't be able to help yourself."

He swallowed. His callused hand caressed her cheek and moved down to her throat. Her skin was as smooth as Stephie's ribbon, only sleeker, warmer. He felt her quiver even at this slight touching from him, and his faint smile mocked her.

For one frozen instant she was still. He leaned over and gently grazed her mouth with his. She was delicious. Warm. Electric. A wildness raced in his blood. She made him ache hotly for everything he had always wanted from a woman and never had. His tongue slid across the edge of her lower lip.

She gasped, and for a second she yielded to the exquisite need he aroused in her, clinging to him hungrily. She ran her hands across the warmth of his muscular chest, twisting her slender fingers into the mat of crisp, golden-brown curls there. Her fingertips hovered in tremulous wonder above the mad excitement of his thudding heart. Nestling closer, she seemed on the verge of giving him all of herself. Then she tensed.

The minute she did, he tightened his arms, forcing her nearer. She bent her head back and sucked in her breath. Very slowly she lifted her hand to his face and traced the shape of his jawline with hot faltering fingertips. Next they explored the curve of his lips.

Again he thrilled to the sensual exploration of her silken touch. Then that mysterious fear came again into her eyes, and she cried softly, struggling to get away from him.

Every male cell felt swollen with arousal.

He let her go. Bewildered, he stared after her as she ran into the house.

What the hell was it with her? She didn't even know who he was, and she was terrified of him. There was no way he could tell her the truth.

And he wanted to.

Five

Christopher was sitting on the porch steps with his forehead buried in his hands, with his frustrated desire burning through him like a brand, when Dallas tiptoed back outside.

"I'm sorry," she whispered on a raw desperate note.

He whirled.

She stood barefoot in the lighted doorway, the masses of gleaming hair flowing over her shoulders like rivers of gold. She faced him rigidly, like a doe at bay, her blue eyes wary, her frightened face without color.

Time stood motionless as those immense velvet eyes caught his.

"I'm sorry." Her voice was softer now.

He knew a real apology when he heard one. He felt flattered, aroused—that, although she was afraid, she cared enough to come back.

"You saved Stephie," she said. "I was unforgivably rude."

"Because I was unforgivably pushy."

Dallas's lashes fluttered against her bloodless cheeks. "There are reasons—"

"So you're haunted by ghosts, too?"

She swallowed hard and nodded.

His mouth thinned.

"Maybe you thought I led you on—by coming aboard your boat," she whispered.

"I thought a lot of things . . . but not that."

"Maybe . . ."

He could see the movement of her breasts through her knit T-shirt. Didn't she know that the taste of her lingered on his lips, that the scent of her still filled his nostrils, that he was still on fire for her? "Let's drop it."

"You seem upset."

Christopher clenched his teeth. "I'm fine."

They lapsed into another of their awkward silences, only after a while, it grew less awkward. She came over and sat on the step below his. The warm silvery darkness and the magic of her nearness seemed to erase all memory of who he really was, of why he had come. Nothing existed outside of this tiny porch and the shimmering night that smelled of damp salt air and the sea. Nothing except this woman. Nothing except the hot, tense excitement she aroused in him. She was a tantalizing mixture of sensuality and innocence. He wanted to know who she was, why she was so determined to run from her ghosts and raise four children who weren't even her own.

Dallas was the first to speak. "Stephie said you rammed the dock this afternoon."

"I just started sailing," he muttered defensively.

"Most people start with little boats. They stay in their own ports."

"I'm not . . . most people. When I have dangerous inclinations, I follow them."

"Such as?"

He stared at her thick, lush, silvery hair, at her slender back, at her narrow waist and perfectly curved bottom. He remembered the hot dark thrill of holding her, and his body tightened. "Like coming here," he murmured quietly.

"You mean setting out on a cruise before you'd mastered sailing?"

He smiled enigmatically. "That. And this, too. Being out here with you."

"I'm not dangerous. You're the one—"

"Oh, but you are—to me."

"Why am I the one who keeps running away?"

"I told you—when I have dangerous inclinations, unlike you, I follow them." His spirits were rocketing sky-high.

"You must lead an exciting life."

"There are those who think so."

"But what do *you* think about your life?"

Nobody had ever asked him that before.

"It's hellishly lonely." He'd been a Hollywood prince, but his low tone was grim as he remembered all the big, perfectly furnished, lonely palaces he'd lived in, all the governesses and servants who'd played Mother and Father, roles his parents had never played. "And I've made a lot of mistakes."

"Because you followed those dangerous inclinations?"

"Partly."

He began to talk about himself. Why had he thought it was hard to talk to her when it was so easy? He found himself telling her about the emptiness of his childhood, telling her hurts he had never confided before. Although he pretended he'd been born into a wealthy ranching family, he stuck to the generalities of his real life, so that he was emotionally truthful. He spoke of his self-absorbed parents, of their neglect. He had been like their pet, not their child. He'd been raised by servants, sent to military schools. He told her how, when he was mad or hurt, he'd done wild stupid things.

She listened, gravely sympathetic, but even as he savored this tenderness, he knew it would vanish the moment she found out who he really was.

When she grew less wary, he asked about her life. She told him about graduate school, about her sister and brother-in-law dying, about giving up her studies to run the marina and raise their children, about missing her intellectual life.

"Surely there was another solution," he said softly, realizing in amazement that they were talking like friends—instead of enemies.

"No. My brother wanted to send them to boarding schools."

Christopher's gaze narrowed. It was going to be one hell of a fight, taking Stephie from her.

Dallas went on talking. "I couldn't let that happen. So, maybe you and I aren't so different. I do these crazy impulsive things that feel right, only sometimes they turn out wrong. But I had to try this." She paused. "My sister helped me once." A look that was pure pain and all grief came into Dallas's eyes. "S-suddenly what I was doing with my own life didn't seem all that important. Not that it's been easy."

"This would be a big job for anybody."

"Just when I think things are under control something awful happens. Like Stephie—tonight." Dallas turned away, upset.

"But I was here," he said gently. *Whose side was he on?*

"Stephie doesn't usually walk in her sleep, but every time Gordon comes, the kids act crazy. Once, Patrick ran away in a dinghy and spent a night on the far shore. Another time, Rennie and Jennie snuck off on motorcycles with the worst boys in their high school. And now Stephie."

His position on the step above Dallas gave Christopher an unrestricted view of her long legs and thighs. He ached to touch her. With a frown he tightened his grip on the railing.

"Sounds like you need a new boyfriend."

"Gordon says that a woman with four kids can't be choosy."

Christopher's heart was pounding again. He forced himself to calm down. "A woman with four kids had better be."

Dallas began to dust her hands on her shorts as if to go. "Look. It's been nice chatting with you Mr.—?".

"Sto—" He caught himself. "Chance." He tried to smile casually.

"Mr. Chance." Her voice was a velvet caress, saying his name.

"The last name's McCall," Christopher drawled.

She got up slowly. "Well, good night, Chance McCall."

He stood up, too. "Don't. Not yet."

She paused, uncertain.

It was difficult making his drawl light and easy as he framed the question that had been on his mind the whole time they'd been talking. "So why did Stephie say that about her birth daddy...coming to take her away?"

Dallas blinked hard and tried to act casual, too. She dusted her hands on her hips again. "I'm sorry you had to hear that. Stephie is a highly emotional child. We don't know where she gets that trait."

Christopher knew.

Dallas hesitated. "Oh, what does it hurt?" She bit her lip. "Stephie just found out she was adopted. It's been very traumatic for all of us."

"She should have been told a long time ago."

"My sister never got around to it. I think she was afraid it might have made a difference since the other children weren't adopted. Then after Carrie died, I thought it best to put off telling Stephie until she got over her grief. I'm afraid she found out the worst way possible."

"How?"

"I was quarreling with..."

He eyed Dallas intently.

"With her biological father. You can't possibly imagine how horrible it was."

Christopher's hard mouth was pressed tightly together. "Try me."

"I didn't know Stephie was listening. She heard just enough so that I had to tell her the truth." Dallas paused. "I shouldn't be burdening you with my problems."

He swallowed. "Somehow they seem like my own."

"You're very kind."

His strong features were absolutely expressionless. "Kindness has nothing to do with it."

"Stephie's always been insecure. It's been pretty upsetting for her to find out she's different than her brothers and sisters. The worst of it is she knows now that her birth father's alive and that he wants her."

"Why is that so bad?" His voice was strangely hoarse.

"He's absolutely dreadful."

"You know him well?" His mouth twisted sardonically.

"I know about him, and I made the mistake of telling her about him. She's been terrified ever since."

Christopher's drawl was low and tense. "Did you deliberately try to make her scared of him?"

"No, of course not. But we've all been through a lot this past year—more than any of us can handle. And now this. She's only six. It's no wonder she can't handle it. I can't, either. Look, I'm sorry. I shouldn't have told you all this. But sometimes . . . it all gets to be too much."

"I understand."

"I want to protect her. But this isn't your problem. It's mine. You probably don't even have kids. Right?"

He felt swift, white-hot fury at this assumption. "Right," he muttered, jamming his fists into his jean pockets.

"But you've been a good listener. Wonderful in fact."

He felt like punching out a windowpane. He might have done something stupid, but he was saved when a piece of furniture crashed upstairs in the children's bedroom and the porch ceiling quivered.

They both glanced up and then at each other. She smiled. "Sounds like I'd better go upstairs now and make sure Stephie really goes to bed."

"I'm coming with you."

"You don't need to."

"I have a vested interest."

She looked genuinely puzzled. The ceiling thudded again as if there were stampeding elephants up there.

He grinned. "Let's just say it's been a helluva long day. I sailed across the bay, rammed the sea wall, tore a chunk out of my foot, saved Stephie, met you. I need my beauty sleep. I want to make sure the little monster really stays put."

Together they went upstairs. Dallas opened her bedroom door just as Patrick screamed, "Gottcha!" and pounded two pillows over Rennie's head. Jennie and Stephie jumped into the frenzy. Patrick's pillow broke and zillions of feathers flew in the icy draft wafting from a window unit.

"Kids, please!" Dallas began helplessly.

The kids kept battling amidst snowing feathers.

"Kids!" Christopher's single word cracked like thunder.

Raised pillows froze in midair, and there was instant silence. Through the falling feathers, four young, worried faces studied the stranger towering in their midst.

"It's bedtime, darlings," Dallas said.

At the sound of their aunt's familiar voice, the kids began chattering madly again.

"Bedtime means silence," Christopher said firmly.

"Not usually," Patrick countered.

"Tonight it does," said Christopher in a tone that brooked no further discussion.

Five minutes later the three older children were in blue bedrolls on the floor. Stephie was curled up in the big double bed by Dallas with a gilt-edged storybook.

"Don't they have their own beds?" Christopher asked, settling himself at the foot of the bed.

"Yes. Their own rooms, too," Dallas said. "But they all sleep with me. I know you must think I spoil them."

"No." He was remembering the loneliness of the big bedrooms he'd slept in as a child. He'd had very little love.

Dallas picked up a couple of storybooks. "It all started when I first came here. We spent the first nights in our own rooms. Then Stephie moved into my bed. Then the others."

Christopher glanced at Dallas. "Stephie sleeps with you—every night?"

"She's been afraid...ever since Carrie and Nick died."

"She's a lucky little girl." He had spoken before he thought. There was a warmth in his eyes and his voice. He was beginning to wonder how he could ever take Stephie away.

"Stephie probably got up...because I went downstairs to wash dishes."

"Would you read me the story about the white horses again, Aunt Dallas?" Stephie asked, handing her aunt the book.

Dallas smoothed the child's hair and began a tale about a white knight with white horses and a white castle who saved a princess from a dragon. There were pictures of the knight splashing about in the surf battling the dragon, of the victorious knight carrying the princess to his castle high on a hill. Stephie was soon so absorbed in the story that she forgot Christopher sprawled across the foot of her bed.

Golden lamplight gleamed in Dallas's fair curls. The twins were sitting on top of their bedrolls French-braiding each other's hair as they listened. A shaggy gray dog's tags jingled as he scratched a flea. Two cats lazed in a corner.

With shining eyes, Patrick crawled up beside Christopher and let Christopher ruffle his soft yellow hair. A cozy familial warmth seeped inside Christopher. He felt better then he had in years—since before Sally died.

When Dallas finished the story, Stephie was asleep. Patrick handed Dallas a comic book that featured *The Tiger,* but she shook her head.

"We always read Stephie's story." The boy stared straight at Christopher. "*The Tiger*'s my favorite!"

Christopher swallowed guiltily.

"Tomorrow night," Dallas promised. "Turn off the light." Patrick was about to object, but Christopher silenced him with a look.

Dallas drew Christopher into the hall. When she shut the door, they were in total darkness. Christopher felt relieved. The cover of Patrick's book had been a publicity still of himself in his mask. Nevertheless, he had felt alarm.

"Stephie loves that story about the horses," Dallas said. "I do, too."

"I thought you weren't the romantic type," he murmured.

"Not in real life. I haven't had much luck with men."

In the darkness she sounded as disillusioned with men as he was with women. Again he wondered why.

"What kind of man do you want?"

"I guess I'm like Stephie. I want the knight with the white horses. Only I'm old enough to know life isn't a fairy tale. There aren't any white knights."

"Maybe because there aren't any princesses worth fighting for anymore." He spoke in a cynical, male, goaded undertone.

"Take my hand," she commanded in a cool voice as if such a comment wasn't what she wanted to hear.

His huge warm hand closed around her delicate fingers. They fit perfectly. As always, her touch was electric. He imagined their bodies fitting together with equal perfection. He longed to draw her into his arms, to lose himself to the sweetness of her warm body in the all-enveloping darkness of the hall. With that thought he brought her fingers to his lips and kissed them. He pulled her to him.

"Don't get the wrong idea," she said, tugging him toward the stairs. "I'm only leading you because I don't want you to break your neck in the dark on a skateboard or something."

"Thanks for bringing me back to my senses," he murmured dryly.

Despite her rejection, a strange, relaxing warmth spread through him as she led him safely past all the obstacles in their path. It seemed to him that he belonged with her in this house, with these children. When they reached the lighted kitchen, he didn't let go of her.

He could see the startled fear in her blue eyes when she glanced down at their entwined fingers. No matter what she might say about her white knight, there was fire in her, desire, warmth—for him. She bit her lips nervously.

"Relax," he whispered.

She yanked her hand free, quickly, too quickly. "How can I with you around?"

"You were good with the kids," he said, attempting to regain his own self-control.

"So were you."

"You sound surprised," he said.

"You don't much look like the fatherly type."

"Why do you keep saying that?"

Her eyes went over his sunburned muscles. At the perfection of his shirtless physique, she drew a deep breath. "You've got that unattached look—no wife, no kids. You've got a boat, your freedom. I've met men like that... who don't want anything else."

"The perfect life." His drawl was very deep, very Texas, and very cynical. "I wish." He was silent. "I'd better go."

But before he could, the screen door was yanked open from the outside. Gordon stormed through it and scowled the instant he saw Christopher. "What are you doing here?"

"Chance was helping me put Stephie to bed," Dallas explained quickly.

"You let *him* go up to your bedroom?"

"She let me do more than that."

Gordon's face went purple.

"Why, she even let me listen to her read a bedtime story."

Gordon whirled on Dallas. "Are you so desperate that any man will do?"

"'A woman with four kids can't be choosy,'" Christopher reminded him ever so softly. "I like kids."

But Gordon didn't hear him because he was already stalking out the door.

"Gordon..." Dallas pushed the door open.

Christopher's large brown hand closed over hers. "Don't chase him, Dallas. That's the worst thing you can do—if you want his respect."

"I was going to apologize."

"You weren't doing anything wrong. He owes you an apology."

Christopher barred the door. He was so close, she had to tip her head back to look into his eyes. Mere inches separated them as he stared down at her with unwavering intensity. They stood for a long moment.

Carefully, oh, so careful not to touch him, she closed the door. "You made him mad on purpose," she accused softly.

"Sometimes I can't help myself."

"Why?"

"I guess I didn't like the way he was treating you. He takes you for granted." Christopher pushed the door back open.

"I thought... maybe you were jealous," she said.

Christopher laughed softly. "Did you want me to be?"

"No! Don't be ridiculous! Of course not!"

"No, of course not," he agreed, but at his quick, mocking smile, she blushed.

"Thanks for what you did and for the advice...about Gordon," she said weakly. "I've made a lot of mistakes with men."

"I've made my share with women," he admitted. "If you're smart, you'll stay away from me."

"So far, you've been kind of hard to avoid."

He smiled sheepishly.

She smiled back. "If you're such a bad news guy, why the warning?"

His white grin broadened. "'Cause I'm not only bad, I'm crazy."

"I don't believe you."

"Really?" He almost laughed out loud. Maybe he was making some progress after all. "Does that mean I'm looking more like a white knight?"

Her gaze touched his broad, sunburned shoulders, the solid wall of his chest, his snug jeans. "I wouldn't go that far." But she blushed again—as if she liked what she saw.

"You were telling me about your mistakes with men."

All her color drained from her face. "I'm divorced."

He considered this and shrugged. "Is that really such a big deal?"

"To me and my family it was."

"Relax. In my case, divorce was the smartest move I ever made," he said grimly. "Everybody gets at least one these days."

Her throat worked convulsively. "Maybe where you come from."

He saw painful memories—her ghosts, he thought—flash briefly in her eyes. "Where I come from, it's the smallest sin." His low voice was gentle. "Not the cheapest, but the smallest."

"Well, it wasn't even my smallest. So how long are you staying?"

"Now that depends," he murmured.

"On what?"

His raspy voice was tensed with emotion. "On you."

She bit her lip and carved a design with her fingernail into the door frame. One minute she was there; the next she wasn't. But long after she had gone he remembered the sad way her lips had twisted and the haunted brilliance of her eyes.

He was more mystified than ever. The more she seemed to like him, the more frightened she became.

Six

Christopher was in a foul mood as he clenched the phone. He wasn't up to dealing with his volatile agent's ranting. Dallas had ignored him ever since he'd saved Stephie.

The noon sun was white-hot dazzle. Rivulets of perspiration trickled down Christopher's spine. He leaned back against the cushions beneath the shade of his blue bimini. Cal's voice buzzed hysterically. Christopher set the phone down and poured himself a cup of ice water, draining it slowly. What he really needed was a swim in the pool.

When he picked the phone up again, Cal was screaming even louder than before. "Have you even heard a word I've said?"

"As few as possible. Look, Cal, I can't come back. Wrap things up for me there, and I'll show up in Spain when they're ready to start filming."

"How in the fungus hell can production start without your insurance physical?"

"These guys'll bend if they have to. Fix it, Cal."

"There's a lot at stake."

Stephie was tiptoeing daintily across wet grass toward the boat with Patrick. She looked very pretty in blue shorts with her black hair blowing loosely in the wind. She leaned down and very carefully picked two pink buttercups.

"Yeah, there's a hell of a lot at stake," Christopher muttered.

"You said you'd be gone no more than a week."

"Has anyone in Hollywood ever lied to you before, Cal?"

Cal groaned. "Fungus! What am I supposed to tell them?"

"Tell them I'm working on my tan."

"How long—"

Dallas came out onto the back porch of her house. At the sight of her in tight jeans and a polka-dot halter top, Christopher felt a hot rush of desire.

"This is complicated, Cal."

"Just tell her who you are and grab your kid and scram."

Dallas looked up and saw Christopher. He waved. Her hands tightened into small fists at her sides. Then she knocked over a planter and became totally flustered rearranging ivy leaves and dirt into her pot before she dashed back inside.

"Like I said, it's complicated."

"I bet if I flew out, I could take care of it in a day."

"No!"

Christopher stared at the screen door that Dallas closed behind her. "This is something I want to handle myself. She doesn't trust me. Any time I act interested in her or her life or her kids, she gets very threatened."

"Smart girl."

"Yeah, she's smart..." his uneasy smile was deeply sensual "...when it comes to books. This may take awhile. I've paid a month's rent in advance."

"A month! Are you crazy?"

"Read the tabloids." Christopher held the phone away from his ear until Cal stopped yelling. "I've got to win her trust so she won't be afraid to give Stephie to me. The best thing I can figure to do is to work at winning the kids first."

Patrick and Stephie had nearly reached the dock.

"And here they are, Cal."

"Don't hang—"

"Sorry, Cal."

Christopher was securing the phone below when Patrick and Stephie came up to the yacht.

"Y'all come on aboard," Christopher drawled, Texas-style.

Patrick shot him an odd look before he jumped aboard. Stephie squatted down and watched them warily from the dock.

"So what's your Aunt Dallas up to this morning?" Christopher asked casually.

"She cooked us pancakes," Patrick said.

"I had cold cereal," Christopher said.

"Great big fluffy ones!" Stephie hollered from the dock, rubbing salt into his wound. "She made homemade syrup, too."

Christopher scowled at them both.

"I guess Aunt Dallas wanted to show off for Gordon," Patrick said.

More salt into an already burning wound. Christopher's grim expression grew darker.

"Only, Gordon sulked and wouldn't eat or speak to Aunt Dallas."

Well, at least there was some good news.

"Hey, guys, how would you like to help me dive for White Horse?" Christopher suggested, to get off the topic of Gordon.

"Who?" Patrick asked.

"It's a stuffed horse Stephie pitched into the drink." Christopher stripped his shirt off.

His sunburn had darkened, and his powerful sinewy muscles were now a deep shade of glistening bronze.

"Wow! You've sure got a lot of muscles," Patrick said. "Like *The Tiger.*"

Christopher's mouth tightened into a forbidding line. Patrick shifted uncomfortably. A look passed between the boy and man. Then without a word Christopher dove into the water. Patrick peeled his shirt off eagerly and jumped in after him. Stephie leaned over the dock and watched their splashes and kicks and bubbles with huge dark eyes. They both dove repeatedly into the muddy brown water. Finally Christopher gave up and hung onto the dock exhausted. Patrick swam over, pulled himself up, too, hanging in a pose that exactly matched Christopher's.

"I—I think I threw him over there," Stephie said pointing toward the stern.

Patrick made two final dives and came up with a dripping lump. He lifted a stringy tail. "Is this him?"

"That's White Horse," Christopher confirmed.

"Poor White Horse," Patrick said laying the pitiful lump on the dock before Stephie. "Just look what you did."

Stephie grew very sad as she studied the sodden animal. Gingerly she touched him on the nose and water squished out of him. "I could hose him off," she offered.

"Would you?" Christopher's voice was very gentle.

She didn't seem to mind when Christopher heaved himself onto the dock and knelt beside her. Nor did she mind when she brushed against his arm as she tenderly hosed White Horse.

She looked up trustingly at Christopher. "Did you like him a whole lot?"

In the past two days, she had become less afraid. "Yes," he murmured, his smile again softening the harsh lines of his face.

"Was he as white as the horses in my storybook?"

Christopher nodded.

"Will he ever be white like that again?"

"Probably not, but we'll have to do our best to take care of him."

"Maybe if we dried him in the oven?" Stephie offered.

"What about your Aunt Dallas?"

"Aunt Dallas wouldn't mind."

But Aunt Dallas *did* mind.

When Christopher strolled into the kitchen as the children's welcome guest, Dallas was in the middle of a tense conversation with Gordon.

Christopher grinned at them boldly. All conversation stopped. Dallas seemed unable to look anywhere but at him, and he, too, grew hotly aware of her. "Do you have a pan we could use to dry our horse?" he asked innocently.

She got up, snatched a pan from a cabinet and banged it down in front of him. "There!"

"Thank you," he purred mockingly.

Dallas was so flustered, she was speechless, but her eyes wouldn't leave Christopher. Without a word, Gordon got up and stalked out. Only when the door slammed behind him, did she flush with embarrassment at the realization that she'd completely forgotten Gordon.

As Dallas rushed belatedly after him, Christopher's lips twitched sardonically. "Not more boyfriend trouble?"

Tense and silent, Dallas stormed back inside. "As if you care."

"You bet I do." With a slow appreciative lift of his brows, his eyes flashed over her with wolfish delight.

Seething, hating the new easiness between the big interloper and her children, she watched Christopher help them adjust the oven.

To retaliate, she sent the children upstairs to change. Christopher was about to go when she attacked. "Do you mind telling me what's so special about that horse?"

She looked mad enough to strangle him. What the hell had he done? Why the hell should he walk around her?

"I'll tell you sometime when you're in a more receptive mood." His low tone was a deliberate insult.

"Tell me now. There's nothing wrong with my mood."

He drew a sharp breath. "Right. You could probably charm the fangs off any rattlesnake." He set his hot insolent gaze on her until she flushed. "Honey, did it ever occur to you that you're not the only one with a temper?" He opened the screen door with a violent gesture and walked out.

Hours later, Stephie came down to the boat with White Horse tucked under her arm.

"Is he dry?" Christopher asked, glancing up from the nautical knot he was practicing tying.

"Almost. I was afraid he might burn."

"That was nice of you to take such good care of him."

"Aunt Dallas says he needs to sit in the sun 'cause he stinks. She told me to bring him down here to you."

At the mention of Dallas, his fingers snapped the line taut. He forced himself to focus on his little girl. "Did she now?" he asked gently.

His stomach was as tight as his knot, but not even the mention of Dallas could spoil this moment for him. This was the first time his child had willingly approached him alone.

"He stinks because you threw him into the saltwater," Christopher said.

"I was scared of you."

"And are you still scared of me?"

Her big dark eyes shone. "No." Then she turned her toes inward just like Sally used to when she was very pleased with herself. "Why's his name White Horse?"

"Another little girl named him that."

"Doesn't she love him anymore?"

"She loved him very much, but she went away and couldn't take him with her."

"Like my mama."

Her face was very still.

His expression was equally grave. "Yes . . . like that. I've been keeping him for her. I think he misses having a little girl to play with."

"I'd play with him," she said wistfully.

"Will you tell him you're sorry you threw him in the water?"

She nestled her forehead against White Horse's damply pungent fur. "I'm sorry, White Horse."

"If you promise to take good care of him, I'll let him stay with you—if I can come up every night and tell him good night."

Again, the big dark eyes met his as she considered his request. Finally she said, "You can come up . . . if you'll read me the story about the white horses."

He wanted to take her in his arms, to kiss her. To tell her he knew what it was to lose someone you loved. Most of all he wanted to tell her who he was, but he didn't want to scare her. So, he held out his hand. She placed her tiny one in his, and they shook on it.

Clutching White Horse to her breast, Stephie withdrew from him and exhaled softly in amazement. Then she skipped all the way back to the house.

That night, when Christopher went to the house to tell Stephie good-night, he secretly hoped to find Dallas reading to the children. He wanted again to feel the warmth of her love for them. But she wasn't there. He read Stephie's story twice, but the whole time he was with Stephie, he grew angry wondering if Dallas was with Gordon. When Christopher went downstairs, he looked for her everywhere.

He was walking by the pool toward the dock when a slim figure moved out of the shadows. "Chance—" Dallas stepped out of the darkness to decorate the night.

A bolt of excitement shot through him. Moonlight turned her hair to silver and made her eyes sparkle. His anger dissolved.

At last she had come to him, and she had deliberately chosen a place where they would have privacy from the children.

Light and shadow emphasized her delicate features, her smooth forehead, her high cheekbones and her slender nose. Her soft, pink mouth was slightly opened. She bit her lips. Then her tongue licked the bitten spot. He ripped his fake glasses off so that he could see her better.

Why did she have to be so incredibly beautiful?

She hesitated. That should have warned him, but instead of being warned, he reached for her and pulled her to him. Their lips met. At first, he thought merely to taste her once. But she was sweet like warm sugar melting against his mouth. One taste, and he was like a starving man ravenous for more.

He was about to kiss her again.

"No!" she cried, beginning to struggle.

He ran his hand under her thin T-shirt, and she trembled, caught between desire, terror and the will to resist. "Honey, this time you came to me." He shaped his hand to her rounded breasts, and her nipples became instantly erect. His own similar response was equally swift and total.

He forgot everything but her. His whole being pulsed with desire. His fingers roamed lower, over her belly, her thighs. The soft texture of her bare skin beneath his calloused fingertips rocked his senses.

Gradually she stilled. Then she arched her body to fit his. Her leg wound around his leg. She was smooth and warm. He felt hot and tightly alive. Skin to skin. Body to body. Male to female. She shaped herself to him. She was sweet wild magic. His arms tightened, and he silently pulled her into the shadows.

Then his mouth covered hers, and fire raced through him. His hands were in her hair, smoothing it against the column of her neck. For weeks she had tormented him. First, by insulting him and refusing to give Stephie to him. Then by driving him crazy with unwanted desire...

His mouth grew hot as he forced her lips apart. His tongue slid into her mouth. "You are beautiful," he breathed. "And sweet. I never expected this."

"Neither did I."

"I wouldn't have come."

"If only you hadn't." A soft tormented sigh escaped her lips.

"How different life would be if humans were granted all their if onlies," he muttered grimly even as his hands mussed her golden hair. "All the shrinks would starve. I had to come."

Suddenly he was a pleasure so intense she couldn't stop her body from melting into his, her arms from stealing convulsively around his neck while her mouth burned against his with equal fire.

He had known passion, but never like this. Her hunger and fevered madness were a perfect match to his. She unleashed all his power, all his wildness. There had been other women in his life; she made him know none of them had ever mattered.

It was a painful shock to them both when she wrenched free.

Her voice trembled. "Stop it. Please... You must—"

He forced his hands to his sides, knotting them in frustration. His breathing was deep.

"This is all wrong," she whispered. "Why am I doing this when I despise you?"

His dark laughter filled the grim blackness of the night. He smoothed his hair that she had tangled with her hands.

"Did you really think you could fool me?" she cried. "That I wouldn't know what a man like you was after?"

He stared at her in shock. *Had she had found him out?*

"I was just playing along with you tonight," she said. "To see how far you'd go with your dirty little game."

"You should have known I'd go all the way."

"You are a scoundrel!"

"The world has already established that fact," he agreed. But his hands were clenched again at his sides.

"To play on children's affections—just to bed me."

When she did not go on, he stared at her in open-mouthed amazement. "Is that all? You mean, you don't really know—"

She was white-faced with anger. He felt faint with relief. She had not found him out after all. "You've got it all wrong, honey," he finished softly.

"Then what was that kiss all about?"

"Come to me any night, and I'll give you a lesson in biology. It's very simple. You want me, and I want you."

"You are a rogue."

"It's more fun to sleep with a rogue than a saint."

"That will never happen."

"Yes, it will, and sooner than you think."

"No!"

His lips curved into a bitter, knowing smile.

"Stay away from me and stay away from my children!"

His eyes blazed into hers with unrelenting determination, but he said nothing.

Only when she backed away and ran stumbling toward the house, did he make a vow in a low inaudible tone.

"No way, lady."

Dallas dashed all the way to her bathroom and locked herself in. She splashed hot water into the tub so the children couldn't hear her sobs and so the steam would cloud the mirror and she couldn't see her face. Then she wept shattering tears of self-loathing.

After years of struggling to redeem herself, of going to church every—no, almost every—Sunday, of burying herself alive on college campuses, of dating safe men, she was still a wanton with dangerous, self-destructive impulses. Why *couldn't* she change?

From the moment she had stumbled onto Chance's boat by mistake, she had known she was lost. Oh, how terribly beautiful he'd been. Right from the first he'd sensed her hunger for his dark powerful body, a longing made fiercer by her years of self-punishing, self-inflicted celibacy. Half-naked in that towel with the planes of chest and his muscular shoulders exposed, he'd been a rampantly virile giant. His brown hair had been overlong and untidy. His brown eyes beneath dark brows, his straight, almost aquiline nose, his high cheekbones and the hard lines of jaw and chin were all set in perfect symmetry.

Even in those ridiculous intellectual-looking glasses that didn't suit him at all, he'd been beautiful. And he knew it. He'd probably never read a book in his life—he hadn't had to. He was physical and direct. She'd been valedictorian of her high school.

He brought it all back—all the pain and the heartache and ruination of so many lives. Why had he come? Why didn't he go? She felt like he was stalking her. She needed to worry about the children and the marina. Instead, thoughts of Chance consumed her.

Hours later, she crawled into bed and fell instantly asleep only to dream her recurring nightmare. As always, she was in that surreal, white, hospital corridor. A baby was crying, as it was being carried away. She was running after it, but its cries grew fainter and fainter. The silence after that was like death. She sprang awake in her bed, her heart pounding with terror.

The air conditioner blasted her with icy air. For a long moment she stared at her bare arms gleaming in the moonlight. Bitter memory replaced the terrible dream. Wearily, she ran her hands through her hair, got up, pulled on her robe and carefully stepped over the hushed children.

Why couldn't she forget? *They had promised her she would forget.* Downstairs she turned on the light, but the familiar clutter of the kitchen seemed like a prison. She snapped the light off again and rushed out into the night.

The moon was low against the water as she headed away from the marina to the beach, and the water glimmered like a flat black mirror. The warm night air was close and humid. Her feet sank into the soft wet sand.

She brushed her hair out of her eyes and stared across the water. Then she sat down on a log that had washed up and hugged her knees to her chest.

A disembodied male voice came out of the darkness and electrified her. "So the ghosts have chased you from your bed, too," Christopher said very softly.

She glanced toward him and sensed that he understood. "I didn't come down here looking for you, if that's what you're thinking."

"It isn't."

"Don't come any nearer," she whispered. "Don't touch me."

"Okay." He held his hands up to show that he was harmless. "Do you mind if the big bad wolf sits down?" His manner was elaborate with gravity.

She considered. His expression was kind. She pointed to the far end of the log. "Not if you sit there."

"That's very kind." He sat down. The still dark silence enveloped them. "Bad dreams?"

She shuddered. "Awful."

"Mine, too." He paused. "Do you want to talk about it?"

"No."

Again he seemed to understand. His low tone was gentle. "Some things are hard to get over."

"Impossible," she said.

"All we can do is try to do better the next time."

"The next time—" She glanced toward him with glittering eyes. "That's the last thing I want."

"Then you're not just running from your past, Dallas. You're running from life."

"Isn't that just a convenient line because you're on the make?"

"Damn." The single word exploded from him.

He got up, coldly furious. For some crazy reason she grabbed his hand. "Please, don't go. That was unfair of me."

His dark eyes met hers.

"Please," she said.

He sat back down.

"I—I know I would be just another woman to you," she said. "I've had that sort of thing before."

His low tone was tense. "Maybe you're wrong about me."

Was she? Doubt tore through her. She moved closer to him, sliding along the log. She brushed her fingers across the back of his hand. Gradually his arm came around her shoulders: gently he pulled her to him. She let her head fall back against his shoulder.

For a long time they sat like that. Until she said, "Chance, I'm afraid of you because of the past."

He looked into her eyes. "You've been crying." A pause. "Because of me?"

She nodded.

"Don't." His hand stroked her tumbled hair. "I'm not worth it. If you're scared, I'll wait."

"You don't understand. I can't ask that. I don't want you wasting your time waiting for me. A long time ago I made a choice about my life, about the kind of person I'm going to be."

"Everything's different now." A pause. "For both of us."

"I won't make the same mistakes again!"

"Let's pray that neither of us do," he said quietly.

She sensed a pain in him that was as pure and all-consuming as her own.

"Chance," she whispered, trying to hold a light rein on her feelings. "I can't let you mean anything to me."

A wicked gleam came into his dark eyes. "Maybe you can't stop yourself." His voice had become thicker and seductively huskier.

"Just because you're handsome, that doesn't mean I'm going to jump into bed with you!"

"So you admit you're attracted?"

"What?"

He grinned. "Honey, I'm going to be your next time. And you're going to be mine."

She shook her head. But she was afraid.

More afraid than ever.

Seven

The next morning, Dallas stood on the pier while Gordon prepared to go. Impatient, she watched him fuss with his auxiliary and radar, coil his lines as he made everything ready. He ordered her about coldly, and she fumbled, displeasing him. He shouted at her while Chance watched them with keen, cynical interest from his own boat.

When Gordon jumped onto the dock to kiss her goodbye, she twisted her face so that his cool lips barely grazed her cheek. Only when she met the dark insolence of Chance's gaze, did she wrap her arms around Gordon with a show of defiant affection and kiss him passionately.

But it was Chance's hot look, not Gordon's kiss, that made her feel she was burning on the inside. Later, as she watched Gordon sail away, she felt only relief. Then her eye caught Chance's amused gaze, and she knew he saw through her like glass.

A dangerous stranger had sailed into her life, and nothing was the same. After that night on the moonlit beach,

Dallas was even more wary of Christopher. She had practically admitted she wanted him. There was now a new closeness between them even though she tried to pretend there wasn't.

Because of Chance, she was more afraid than ever of the latent sensuality in her nature, and she feared any similar tendency in the twins. But while Dallas began smothering her figure with layers of clothing, the girls stripped down to bikinis. Every time she saw their bare brown midriffs, she carried out their cover-ups.

Dallas had more nightmares. Only now when she woke up, she was afraid to go out. Once, however, the terrible feelings so overpowered her that she sneaked out at dawn. When she came to the marina, Chance was there in the darkness, his great body lounging negligently against a piling. His white shirt was open and fluttering, and her eyes were drawn like a magnet to his smooth tanned skin underneath.

They didn't speak, but she felt funny little dartings of sensation in her stomach as she hung there with an insane, suicidal desire to run her fingertips up and down his brown skin, knowing that he would welcome her into his arms. Maybe when she knew the rapture of his lovemaking, she could forget the pain that had haunted her for years. But when he started boldly toward her, her knees began to shake. She stared at him for a frozen second. Then she cried out and raced past him.

It didn't help that the kids adored him. Patrick and he were great friends. The boy had taught Chance to skateboard while Chance had taught him to board sail. Rennie and Jennie were crazy about him, too, and were constantly on his boat in their bikinis, which Dallas imagined Chance enjoyed immensely.

Dallas pleaded with them to stay away from him, but they wouldn't listen. Then one afternoon the girls picked the wrong time to saunter through the kitchen in their bikinis on their way to his boat. Dallas had just burned her pie crusts when she heard the twins' giggles on the stairs.

They flounced through the kitchen carrying towels and their boom box. "Hi, Aunt Dallas—"

Through the haze of smoke Dallas saw long slim legs, wiggling breasts and bottoms. Her smoking crusts tumbled into the trash.

"Girls!"

They stopped, their expressions instantly sulky.

"Where are you two going...dressed, or should I say undressed, like that?" Dallas asked.

"What's wrong with the way we're dressed?" Rennie taunted.

Dallas went over and tugged Rennie's bra strap higher, but that just left more nubile flesh hanging out below. "You seem to have outgrown your costumes."

"You never cared before Mr. McCall came," Rennie said, yanking her suit back down.

"I want you both to change."

"You have a dirty mind," Rennie said.

"And Mr. McCall's is as pure as the driven snow?" Dallas said.

Both girls nodded hopefully.

"Give me a break! If you believe that, you have a lot to learn about men."

Their faces were eager for such knowledge.

"Not that I want you learning any of it any time soon. Either you change, or you help me in the kitchen."

"Why are you so old-fashioned?"

"Believe it or not, we had sex back in the olden days."

"I bet you never did," Rennie accused.

Dallas went pale.

"She's just jealous," Jennie said slyly.

"Yeah," Rennie cut in. "You sneak out at dawn when you know he'll be out there."

"He knows you like him," Jennie said. "He's always asking us about you."

"Girls!" Dallas's stern tone stopped them. "I won't listen to any more of this."

"Well, we're not going to listen to you about him, either."

On that belligerent note they bounded upstairs. When they came back down, they were more sullen than ever, but at least they were covered by voluminous T-shirts.

Dallas's victory was short-lived. An hour later she saw them sprawled across Chance's foredeck on their stomachs wearing nothing except their bikinis—with the tops undone!

The only good thing was that Chance was in the water rigging the sailboard for Patrick. Even after Patrick sailed away and the girls called to him, Chance did not go to them. He waited until Patrick fell and then swam out to him.

Dallas couldn't let the twins get by with such behavior. She had to talk to Chance. So, when the girls left that afternoon to visit friends, Dallas marched down to his boat. Naturally, he was so conceited, he misinterpreted everything.

The instant he saw her, his gaze roamed her shapely length. "I'd almost given up waiting for you to come," he said softly, as he sprang lithely to the dock and grabbed a line with a tanned arm to pull the boat nearer so that she could climb aboard more easily.

His every movement brought the play of his darkly tanned muscles. Wary, she shrank from him. "Don't you dare think I came because I wanted to."

He took her hand, and even this casual touching caused a tingle of excitement to sweep through her.

"Okay. I won't dare." His eyes twinkled with amusement as he turned her hand over in his palm. "Nevertheless, I'm glad you're here," he purred warmly.

"I told you, it's not like that."

"Right." He helped her aboard. "You've been on my mind a lot lately. No woman has ever driven me crazier."

"And I suppose a lot of women chase you." The thought was so unpleasant that she frowned.

"I've had my share, but you don't have to worry." His alert brown eyes touched her mouth and her breasts with a suggestive look that sent hot color rushing to her cheeks. "I like to do my own chasing." He grinned wickedly. "You're more my type."

"You're saying you're the kind of predator who likes to stalk his own prey. That's hardly reassuring."

"I don't think those were my exact words," he murmured dryly. "Would you like a drink?"

She sank onto a cushion as he leaned over the ice chest. "This isn't a social call," she said primly.

"Does that have to mean we can't enjoy ourselves?"

"I came because of the twins. Please, leave them alone."

He straightened abruptly. "Don't you have things backward?" The faintest edge had come into his voice. "They're the ones who come down here and bother me."

Throwing caution away, she persisted, "You seem to enjoy them."

His tone was grimmer. "I like kids."

"There's more to it than that."

"Like what?"

"They're not exactly kids. They're young women." Dallas drew a sharp little breath. "I want you to stop encouraging them."

Christopher's hand clamped around her arm and hauled her to her feet. "Just what are you accusing me of?"

"They're too interested in you."

His hard hand tightened, and, as always, when she came into physical contact with him, she lost the ability to think. It had been a dangerous stunt to come down here and confront him.

He drew her closer. His handsome face was a chiseled mask, but she sensed he was deeply angry. His body was like living muscular bronze. Suddenly, everything was reduced to some primitive level that made her feel dominated by him.

"Is that my fault?" he muttered roughly. "Their father's dead. They're at a boy-crazy age."

"You're taking advantage of their innocence."

"How?"

"You're deliberately attracting them."

"Elaborate," he snapped.

"You've been too clever. You know I can't."

"Because I'm not doing a damn thing."

In silence he regarded her for a long charged moment. Finally he said, "There's only one woman around here I want to attract. Only one woman I'm tempted to take advantage of." Dark furious fires blazed in his eyes. "The twins know it. I know it. And you know it. Maybe that's the real reason you came down here—to tempt me."

Dallas's heart went to her throat. She'd aroused a beast she was now helpless to control. "You know it isn't."

"I don't know any such thing, but why don't you show me—now—exactly what your feelings for me are."

She struggled to free his hand from her arm, but that only made him angrier. His hands tightened into a bruising vise. He dragged her against the lean hardness of his body, and his mouth covered hers in a long, punishing kiss. Her trembling hands reached up to push him away. But when they encountered solid muscle, they gave up and wound limply around his neck.

He pulled her closer and held her tighter until their bodies fused. "Don't fight me, honey. There's no way you'll win."

Desire sizzled through her like a jolt of electricity. If he was hot, he made her hotter. This was what she longed for when she lay awake. Her tongue dipped inside his mouth

The more
you love romance . . .
the more
you'll love this offer

FREE!

Mail this heart today! (See inside)

Join us on a Silhouette® Honeymoon
and we'll give you
4 Free Books
A Free Victorian Picture Frame
And a Free Mystery Gift

IT'S A
SILHOUETTE HONEYMOON—
A SWEETHEART OF A FREE OFFER!
HERE'S WHAT YOU GET:

1. Four New Silhouette Desire® Novels—FREE!

Take a Silhouette Honeymoon with four exciting romances—yours FREE from the Silhouette Reader Service™. Each of these hot-off-the-press novels brings you the passion and tenderness of today's greatest love stories…your free passports to bright new worlds of love and foreign adventure.

2. A Lovely Victorian Picture Frame—FREE!

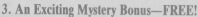

This lovely Victorian pewter-finish miniature is perfect for displaying a treasured photograph. And it's yours FREE as added thanks for giving our Reader Service a try!

3. An Exciting Mystery Bonus—FREE!

With this offer, you'll also receive a special mystery bonus. It is useful as well as practical.

4. Convenient Home Delivery!

Join the Silhouette Reader Service™ and enjoy the convenience of previewing 6 new books every month delivered right to your home. Each book is yours for only $2.49* per book, a saving of 30¢ each off the cover price plus only 69¢ delivery for the entire shipment! If you're not fully satisfied, you can cancel any time, just by sending us a note or shipping statement marked "cancel" or by returning any shipment to us at our cost. Great savings plus convenience add up to a sweetheart of a deal for you!

5. Free Insiders' Newsletter!

You'll get our monthly newsletter packed with news on your favorite writers, upcoming books, even recipes from your favorite authors.

6. More Surprise Gifts!

Because our home subscribers are our most valued readers, when you join the Silhouette Reader Service™, we'll be sending you additional free gifts from time to time—as a token of our appreciation.

START YOUR SILHOUETTE HONEYMOON TODAY—
JUST COMPLETE, DETACH AND MAIL YOUR FREE-OFFER CARD

START YOUR
SILHOUETTE HONEYMOON TODAY.
JUST COMPLETE, DETACH AND MAIL YOUR
FREE-OFFER CARD.

If offer card below is missing write to:
Silhouette Reader Service,
P.O. Box 609, Fort Erie, Ontario L2A 5X3

**Business
Reply Mail**

No Postage Stamp
Necessary if Mailed
in Canada

Postage will be paid by

SILHOUETTE READER SERVICE™
P.O. Box 609
Fort Erie, Ontario
L2A 9Z9

DETACH AND MAIL TODAY!

and ran hungrily along the edge of his teeth. He groaned aloud, and she grew aware of the passionate tremors wracking his body. There was suction on her tongue, and he pulled it deeper into his mouth until she was without breath, without life, without even the will to fight.

At last he ended the drugging kiss. His lips lifted a fraction of an inch. His moist warm breath flowed against her mouth. Her long-lashed eyes fluttered open.

Tenderly his hand brushed tangled gold wisps away from her cheek. "Why do you always think the worst of me?"

"Anybody can see us out here...like this," she whispered. Then she looked past him and found her worst fears realized. Both twins were sitting on the porch railing staring out at the marina. "Oh, dear, the twins—"

"I thought you wanted me to let them know I'm not interested in them," he murmured.

"This wasn't exactly the way I had in mind."

"All we did was kiss."

"Why did it feel like so much more?"

His enigmatic smile was tender. "You know why."

"They'll think I'm a hypocrite," she said weakly.

"You're a woman."

That was the problem.

She started to move away, but Christopher captured her chin to hold her still. Then with languorous slowness, his mouth touched hers. Like a hotly burning flame, his lips moved fleetingly across the satiny softness of her mouth once more before he let her go.

"You're an incredibly beautiful woman. We haven't done anything wrong," he said.

"Will my life ever be like it was? Are you ever going to sail away?"

He stepped in front of the sinking sun, and his long shadow fell darkly across her face. His eyes devoured her. "Only after I've gotten what I came for. And, Dallas, I'm running out of time. We need to talk."

"No—I can't. The restaurant will open in an hour."

"Then when?"

"I don't know."

"You can't put me off forever."

But she could try.

With a shaking hand Dallas was outlining her lips with lipstick. She nearly dropped the tube when she heard a man's heavy stride on the front porch.

Gordon was never early. He was always precisely on time.

She dashed to the upstairs window and peeked through the miniblinds expecting Gordon. Instead, the porch light was gleaming on Chance's brown hair. When he glanced up, she jumped back from the window. Then she turned on the twins who began suddenly brushing their hair innocently.

"What's he doing here?" Dallas demanded, putting the cap on her lipstick and thrusting it into her purse.

"You called Gordon. We called Chance."

Dallas snapped her purse shut. "I thought you agreed not to chase him."

"When we told him you were going out, he offered to baby-sit. I thought it was very sweet of him."

"Sweet?" Dallas almost shrieked the word. "You girls are teenagers. You're perfectly capable of baby-sitting."

"But Chance said he was concerned—that you were leaving us all alone."

"I'll just bet he was."

The calculating nerve of that clever, handsome devil.

Still, Dallas felt a quick twinge of guilt. She had begged Gordon to let her bring the children with her so that they could get to know him better, but he had refused.

"Chance said this place is pretty remote," Jennie explained, defending him.

Dallas picked up her brush. "For heaven's sake, we run a public restaurant."

"He told us that makes it even more dangerous," Rennie said. "Anybody could drive up."

Dallas was yanking the brush through her hair. "Why can't you see Chance is just taking advantage of this situation?"

"How?" both girls wanted to know.

"Why did you call Gordon, when it's Chance you really like?" Jennie asked before Dallas could answer.

"Because . . . I mean . . ." Dallas flushed guiltily.

"Ever since we saw you kiss him, you keep trying to pretend you don't like him," Jennie insisted.

"Why, that's pure poppycock," Dallas said. But her voice was unsteady.

"Poppy what?" Stephie demanded brightly from the doorway.

Dallas turned beet red. She set her brush firmly back down on the bureau and drew a deep calming breath. "Forget it," she said calmly. "Look, girls . . . I've known Gordon for years. He *is* my boyfriend."

"But he's so boring," Rennie said.

Stephie had came into the room. "And he doesn't like us."

"Of course he does."

"Then why doesn't he talk to us and play with us the way Chance does?"

Because he doesn't stoop to playing on children's emotions to get what he wants!

Instead of answering, Dallas pressed her lips tightly together and took another deep breath.

"And he never kisses you the way Chance kissed you." Rennie sighed romantically. "Chance is *so* cute."

"There's more to relationships than . . . than . . . that sort of thing," Dallas said sharply.

All three girls looked deeply puzzled. Then Stephie said with an air of immense wisdom, "When the prince kissed the princess like that in my storybook, it was the best part. They got married and lived happily ever after.''

"That was a fairy tale. This is real life.''

"I like the fairy tale better,'' Stephie said.

Dallas was at a loss to reply. Fortunately Chance's firm knock resounded against the wooden door. All three girls rushed downstairs to welcome him. Dallas reluctantly followed them. When she stepped into the living room, Chance was already surrounded by all four children. He was dressed in jeans, boots and a Western shirt made of pale blue cotton. His immense silver belt buckle caught the light and flashed at her. Stephie was telling him excitedly that Gerry, their gerbil, had gotten loose from his cage.

"We'd better find him before Harper and T.C. pounce on him and eat him for dinner,'' Chance said.

"I like your boots,'' Patrick said.

Chance awkwardly lifted one foot, and Patrick knelt down to study the boot's elaborate stitching. "They feel kind of narrow in the instep,'' Chance said.

"We cooked chocolate-chip cookies,'' Rennie and Jennie said.

"My favorite,'' said Chance.

He certainly had a way with kids.

Over the three golden heads and Stephie's dark one, Chance's brown eyes met Dallas's. He tucked his thumbs in his belt loops and leaned against the couch. Her nerves vibrated in response to his easy warmth.

He had a way with women, too, whispered a treacherous secret voice that Dallas was determined to ignore.

"You didn't have to come,'' Dallas said.

A slow smile spread across his strong sensual mouth. "I wanted to.''

His virile charm was working its magic on her. The pale blue of his crisp collar emphasized his tan. Denim molded his thighs like a second skin. His ridiculous spectacles only made him more adorable. He shook his head slightly so that his silken hair would fall away from his eyes.

Nervously Dallas turned and saw the casual clutter of skateboards, half-filled glasses, dirty plates, discarded clothes and paperback books. "Kids, you know how much Gordon hates messes." She stopped when she met Chance's hard, mocking gaze. She stooped to pick up a pair of Patrick's dirty socks.

"Patrick, get your sneakers," Chance ordered quietly. "The rest of you pitch in. We want to help your aunt make a good impression on her boyfriend." Despite the smoothness of his response, there was the faintest challenge in his taunting drawl.

"We do?" This was a new concept to all the kids.

Dallas flushed. Thank goodness Chance didn't allow them to debate the point. With his help the room was soon immaculate.

When they finished, Dallas felt awkward being alone with Chance and the kids. Chance kept looking at her, not saying anything and yet communicating a fierce tension that made her feel guilty. At last when the children went into the kitchen, he said, "The kids told me you called Gordon."

"What if I did?"

"If you were lonely, you should have come to me."

"Who said you can give me what I want?"

His glance was dark and unsmiling. "What exactly are you looking for?"

"That's my business."

"I'm making it mine." He spoke between his teeth.

Her voice grew saccharine sweet. "I thought you came over to baby-sit."

His mouth thinned. "That was only one of my reasons."

When the kids came back into the room, the atmosphere was almost volcanic. In the tense confusion, she escaped to the restaurant to check on Pepper and Oscar. Since it was Tuesday, there weren't many customers. Oscar was listening to Mexican polkas while he sliced potatoes, and Pepper was flirting with a rancher. Because she knew Chance was back at the house, Dallas lingered, folding napkins, filling water glasses as she talked to Oscar. Only when she saw Gordon's car pull up in front of the house, did she rush back. She opened the door, and both men leaped from the couch to their feet.

"Doesn't she look beautiful?" Chance's voice was rich and low.

She knew he was furious that she was going out with Gordon, but he concealed his anger with a skillful facade of easy charm. For a rancher, he was a superb actor. Her cheeks grew redder the longer Chance studied her with that possessive hot look that somehow implied she was his.

Why did he have to be so impossible—so arrogantly possessive, so difficult and somehow so dangerous? She had a right to call whomever she wanted, didn't she?

Why did she have to be so drawn to him?

"She does look beautiful," Gordon agreed unenthusiastically.

"Thank you." It was hard to be civil when she was furious at both of them. Anxious to go, she stepped toward the door.

There was a clumsy scuffle of boots on hard wooden flooring as Chance tripped over his pointed toes in his rush to open the door for her. When he lurched into her, he grinned foolishly, charmingly. Then his dark gaze raked over her with lingering intensity.

"You two have fun," he murmured.

Despite the hint of cynicism in his twisting mouth, she sensed some deeper emotion just beneath the surface.

"We will," she snapped. "Watch yourself in those boots. For a rancher, you seem a little unsure in them."

A dark flush stole across his face. He didn't even attempt a smile. "I haven't broken them in yet."

Defiantly, she thrust her hand into Gordon's.

Gordon took her to The Blue Diamond, her favorite seafood restaurant, but she couldn't concentrate on the food or Gordon. Instead, she kept wondering what Chance and the kids were doing. It was almost pleasant to imagine the kids wrecking the house and driving him as crazy as they drove her.

Hours later when Gordon pulled up to the house, the first thing she saw were four motorcycles gleaming darkly in the moonlight.

Dear Lord. Not Rodge and Stew again, and the rest of their worthless pack. Dallas had forbidden the girls to associate with them after that night when they'd ridden off with them.

The minute Gordon braked, she jumped from the car and flew past the bikes to confront Chance and the twins. Chance must have heard her because he pushed the door open from the inside. His face instantly hardened as he saw the wild panic in her eyes.

"What's wrong?" he demanded. He looked past her and saw Gordon's grim look. "Did that bastard try..."

"It's not Gordon, you idiot," she whispered. "It's you. I should have known I couldn't trust you with my children."

"What the hell have I done now?"

She burst into the living room expecting to discover bedlam only to find the four teenage boys grouped around the television eating popcorn and watching a golf tournament. The twins were in the kitchen cleaning up. That was a first. And they were modestly dressed in baggy jeans and huge T-shirts. Patrick and Stephie were watching a recaptured Gerry race on top of the wheel in his cage. The house was even cleaner than when she'd left. She could never have managed eight kids so well.

"It's a good thing I was here," Chance spoke softly from behind her. "Rodge and Stew came over right after you left. I'm not sure the twins could have handled them."

Dallas knew from experience that they couldn't. Not that she would admit that to Chance.

"It's good for boys to know there's a man in the house," Chance said.

He said it as if he felt he belonged.

"I'm glad you were here," Dallas admitted reluctantly. Then Gordon walked in.

The lamplight shone in her hair, on her face. Her gaze grew radiant as she looked at Chance. She didn't even see Gordon.

"Hey, hi there—" This, from her date.

Chance and Dallas turned.

Dallas forced a polite smile. "Oh?"

"Dallas, why don't you come outside and tell me good-bye?" Gordon said stiffly.

"Okay." But her eyes flicked briefly back to Chance before she left.

Outside, at his car, Gordon took her hand. "So, it's over."

"Over?"

"Us. It's you and this muscle-bound, McCall, nut case now."

"No—"

Gordon turned her hand over. "Maybe you can't admit it yet. But I know it. And McCall damn sure knows it. He already acts like he owns you. I was afraid he might strangle me when I came over to pick you up."

"If he said anything—! If he so much as touched a hair on your—"

"No! Look, you deserve to be happy, Dallas. Don't fight him too long. He doesn't know beans about sailing, or ranching, or boats, but he's got money from somewhere or he wouldn't have a yacht like that and time off. Not many men would look at a woman with four kids. And a motor-cycle gang, too! The guy's crazy.''

"By his own admission.''

Gordon smiled, and she reached up and kissed his cheek. He got into his car, and she watched until his red taillights blurred with the other lights on the causeway bridge.

Chance came out onto the porch and stepped under the light. "Where's your date?"

"As if you didn't know.''

Chance stuck his thumbs in his belt loops and waited for her to explain. "Well? Is it too much to hope that he's gone for good?''

She stepped onto the porch. "Thanks to you!''

His mouth curved sardonically. "Oh, so it's my fault?''

Dallas nodded.

"And you're furious?'' Chance studied her expression. "I can see you're set on keeping me guessing. Does this mean we can see more of each other?''

"I don't think that's wise.''

"Why?''

"Gordon was safe. You're not.''

"Some women are attracted to danger.''

"I was—once. A long time ago I knew someone like you.''

"Your ex?''

She was very still. "No. Before him.'' She broke off.

"Who?''

Her throat thickened. She looked away to the silken rip-ple of the water and the silver gleam of the masts. "I don't want to talk about him.''

The silence grew awkward until his deep voice filled it. "Neither do I. Let's talk about us. I want you to stop being scared. I'm not that guy who hurt you. I want to be your friend.''

"No.''

"Hell, you're right." Thumbs came out of his belt loops. He reached over his head and unscrewed the light bulb. The porch melted into darkness as he pulled her closer. She struggled, but his arms were tight. He locked their bodies together as perfectly as the last two matching pieces of a puzzle. His legs were long and muscled, his thighs like iron. His husky tone made her shiver. "I've never been the kind of man who can settle for less when I want more."

"Chance—"

He brought his warm fingertip to her lips. "If I keep letting you run the show, I'll never get anywhere." He lowered his head and nuzzled her hair with his lips. "Honey, I don't just want to be friends. I want you. And not just for sex. I think I could care about you in a way I've never cared about anyone."

His mouth crushed down on hers, and he kissed her until she could hardly breathe. His big flexible hands shaped her to him. He was hot, so hot, and he made her hot for him, too. It no longer mattered that they were strangers. They seemed to belong together. He had only to look at her, to touch her, and she was instantly on fire. The powerful heat of his body and the slight roughness of his hands on her skin tantalized her.

"Come to my boat," he whispered in a hoarse low tone.

She reached up and put her fingers across his lips.

He pushed her fingers away. "Dallas, come to me after the boys go home and the kids are in bed. We don't have to make love. I just want to be with you. I can't wait much longer." The sky was a haze of stars, silvered by moonlight. "Promise me," he demanded.

He held her a long time, his body pressing into hers, not letting her go, the torrid warmth of him seeping deep inside her. Why was she silent when she knew she had to say no?

His lips were in her hair again. "Maybe if I had more character, I'd sail away and leave you alone."

She brushed his brown hair away from his forehead. "I'm beginning to think that you're not such a bad guy."

"Hey, where did that strap of sweetness come from?"

She touched his cheek, mutely pleading for him not to ask what she wasn't ready to give. In the darkness his features seemed harsher and bleaker than ever. She sensed a loneliness in him, a need for her that transcended the physical.

"Come to me," he murmured.

She remembered another man, and another night, and the tragedy that had followed. "No."

"Right."

Chance's hot wild lips touched her mouth angrily again and enflamed her; her response was a quick, needy fever that enthralled him. With skilled lips and hands, he took a long time over their wanton embrace. When he let her go, she sagged limply against the darkened wall of her house, her skin so flushed and hot she felt she'd die if she didn't have him.

She was infinitely sad.

"You could at least smile." Chance's voice broke the silence that seemed to engulf them.

"No. I can't even give you that."

Eight

A lonely gull soared against a flame-colored sky. When the wake of a passing tug slapped the hull of Christopher's yacht, he sprang awake instantly.

He was alone, his every muscle taut after a restless night on his bunk. He poked his head out of the hatch. There wasn't a breath of a breeze. He dragged his fingers through his hair and stared at the untouched pillow beside his.

She hadn't come.

He slammed his fist into fiberglass. Pain shot from his knuckles all the way to his elbow.

Damn it, he could have his pick of women. She didn't even know who he was, yet she had that edge as if she intuitively sensed the danger of him.

If he'd been in L.A, he could have raced his Jaguar up and down along the Pacific headlands. He would have watched the raging surf dash itself against the rocks. Here, he felt caged in, trapped. He wanted to step out of the role he was playing and be himself. No more brown contacts, no more brown hair, no more glasses.

No more lies.

He wanted to be Christopher Stone, Stephie's father, Dallas's lover.

He picked up his phone and dialed Cal.

"What do you mean, no progress?" Cal roared, awake instantly, despite the early hour. "This woman who can keep the Tiger at bay, I've got to meet. Why don't you just tell her who you are?"

No more lies.

"I've got to win her first."

"Tell her."

"Three-time losers shouldn't give advice to the love-lorn."

"Then why'd you call?"

"I had to talk to someone. I had to quit pretending—if only for five minutes. Everybody's asleep here."

"It's 4:00 a.m. What the hell do you think I was doing—saying my prayers?"

"You're my agent."

"Not at this fungus hour."

Cal hung up.

It was a first.

Still restless, Christopher picked up his script and began to go over it.

Later when he went to the house, he was told that Dallas had driven into the city and wasn't expected back until late.

She had run away.

He was furious, but he'd go mad if he thought about her. He decided to work. Then Oscar turned his television on so loud in his houseboat that Christopher couldn't think. He stuffed the script into a bag and stalked with it down the beach.

It was almost dark when he returned, but Oscar's television was still blaring. Dallas's Jeep was parked in front of her house. Other cars were lined up at the restaurant. It looked like a busy Wednesday. Why the hell was Oscar's television still on if he was over there cooking?

Christopher decided to check. Oscar's "houseboat" was a rusting trailer on top of a wooden barge with old tires nailed to the sides. Carefully, Christopher picked his way across the littered deck—ice coolers, crab nets, old air conditioners and fishing paraphernalia.

He cracked open the door. The first thing he saw were the opening credits for *Tiger Three* blazing across the television screen.

Christopher's stomach tightened. If Dallas recognized him, he was dead.

Oscar was sprawled across his tattered couch. His stained T-shirt had ridden up his hairy belly. Four dozen beer bottles were lined up along the edge of his coffee table. The houseboat reeked of cheap booze and cigarette smoke.

Christopher slammed the door. Nothing. He strode inside and switched off the set. With a groan, Oscar rolled over. Christopher picked up a beer bottle and flipped it into the trash can. He pitched in more bottles, so that they broke noisily on top of the other. More groans and snores from the couch.

"Oscar—" Dallas's voice was silken.

At the sound of it, Christopher's hand jerked, and the next bottle shattered against the wall.

Dallas's bright head peered inside. "You missed."

He turned. "Right." His gaze drifted down the delicate line of her jaw, the slim column of her neck. Why did just looking at her make him feel so warm he was burning? "Funny, till I met you, I usually got what I aimed for."

Her indrawn breath was followed by an electric silence.

Christopher's hot gaze licked over her shape like lightning. Her hair hung down along one side of her face like a shimmering veil of gold. She wore an apricot jersey dress that clung to every curve. "So you're back?"

Her breath seemed to catch in her throat again. Her fragile poise seemed eggshell thin. But, then, so was his.

"I like your dress," he murmured in a voice that was as dry as dust. "Is it new?"

Warm color came and went just under the surface of her golden skin. "I—I bought it today."

"So you went shopping?"

She flushed again.

"Funny, I thought you were just avoiding me."

Her shaky hand pushed her hair behind one ear. "That's because you're so conceited you think the world revolves around you."

That stung. "Right. You've got me completely figured."

"You don't own me," she said.

"Not yet—anyway."

She went white. "Where's Oscar?"

"See for yourself."

As Christopher swaggered insolently toward her, she unconsciously clenched the door frame for support. Pushing the door wider, he stepped aside so that she could see past him.

Oscar snorted loudly. His filthy T-shirt rode higher, revealing more of his black-haired belly.

Dallas went numb. "What am I going to do?" she asked in a low, forlorn tone.

She moved into the light, and Christopher saw the shadowy smudges of exhaustion beneath her eyes. She was trying to run this place and raise four kids. Her shoulders drooped.

He forgot his own frustration. Before he thought, he said, "I'll cook."

"No!" She drew herself up primly. "I couldn't dream of bothering you—"

"Lady, all you do is bother me."

"I've managed alone before."

He stared at her for a long moment. "I bet it was hell."

"No—"

His gaze darkened. "Some things are hard to do alone."

She backed away from him until she stumbled into the wall. "Why are you such a hard man to say no to?"

When he grinned with new hope, she stiffened.

"Relax, sweetheart. You're not selling your soul to the devil."

"I—I suppose I could hire you—for one night only."

"Oh, I don't want money." His wicked grin flared again. "And I'll never be satisfied with one night only."

"Then what are you doing it for?"

He laughed softly. "The white knight to the rescue."

She was instantly unnerved. "You're no white knight, and if you refuse money, I won't owe you . . . anything else."

He felt a violent rush of physical desire. "I don't ever work for nothing. White knights carry off their princess."

"You are insufferable."

"Chalk it up to knightly charm."

She stared at him one second longer. Then she bolted through the door.

Christopher followed after her at a leisurely pace. When he discovered the twins fighting in the dining room, he set them to sweeping and arranging tables and chairs. He found Patrick hiding in the house watching *Tiger Three*.

Christopher's stomach tightened as he switched off the set. "We need you in the restaurant."

"Aw! The best part was coming next!"

"Yeah, I know."

Patrick's sharp eyes flicked over Christopher's features and narrowed assessingly. Uncomfortable, Christopher pushed his glasses higher up his nose.

Patrick started to say something and stopped. A telling look passed between the boy and man. Without another word they went to the restaurant.

Despite Dallas acting nervous every time Christopher came near, he enjoyed working with her immensely. He cooked while she took orders, and the night went well. It was as if he was part of a team, part of a family. The kids were enthusiastic to please him. If only Dallas hadn't been so jumpy, everything would have been perfect. But when he came into a room, she left it.

When the last customer had gone, the kids were cleaning up the kitchen, and Dallas was standing behind the cash register, tallying receipts. It was a hot night. A damp sheen of perspiration made her skin glow.

Christopher went over and leaned heavily across the counter. "You're too pretty to be a scholar of metaphysical poetry. Too pretty for a dump like this, too. I could take you away from all this."

She drew back, startled.

"Let me help you with those."

She set down the bills and placed her hand on top of them. "You've already done too much." When he didn't budge she said, "Look, it's late. I'm tired. You're tired."

"Right. We've both got going to bed on our minds."

"Don't start that! Please . . ."

"You're wrong about me," he murmured in a more serious tone.

"I don't think so."

"We could have a beer on my boat. You might say thank you."

"No—to a beer on your boat." She flipped through the receipts. "Yes—to thank you." Softly. "Thank you. . . ."

"I'd like a *private* thank-you," he said, leaning closer.

"I know what you'd like."

"We could just talk."

"You want more."

His hand slid beneath her chin. "Right. So do you."

She shook her head, moving away from him.

"Damn it, Dallas. Why are you so dead set against me?"

Her blue eyes were unsmiling. "I told you. I've been burned in the past. I'm not quite as naive as I was back

then.'' She paused. ''All right, if you really want to know.
You don't add up, Mr. McCall. You're a rancher, but you
never talk about ranching. You can't even walk in cowboy
boots.''

''I told you they were new.''

''Your accent's funny.''

''What the hell's wrong with it?''

''It's just different.''

''So—I wasn't born in Texas.''

''There are other things. You sailed over here, but Gordon says you don't know how to sail.''

''How the hell does he know? He's never seen me.''

''That's just it. You never take your boat out.''

''Maybe I like it here.''

''You have a big boat, but Gordon says you don't know
anything about it.''

''Just because I'm not a talking engine manual like that
nitpicky big-mouth—''

''Look, forget Gordon.''

''With pleasure!''

''You're a handsome guy. You could have anyone. Yet
you take an interest in me, in my kids.''

Christopher shrugged. ''So, I like you and your kids.''

''That's unusual. You're not a relaxed kind of guy who
just sails off into the sunset and leaves everything behind. I
keep asking myself. Why here? Why my kids? Gordon said
no man—''

Suddenly Christopher was very angry. Angry that she was
using his lies to paint him into a corner; angrier, though,
that no matter what he did, he got nowhere with her. ''I
thought we agreed to forget that jerk!'' He paused. ''You
know what your problem is—you've stuck your head inside books so long, you don't know the first thing about
life.''

''I know that you scare me, and I'm not sure why.''

He felt explosive. "Maybe if you came down to my boat and got to know me a little better, you could figure it all out. Would it be such a crime to give us a chance?"

Before she could answer, he stalked out. He was aware of the kids watching him. One of them knocked a glass over, and he heard it shatter behind him. The twins ran over to Dallas.

"Chance—" Dallas called after him desperately.

He stopped, hesitating when he saw her stricken expression. But she said nothing more. If she'd come halfway—

When she didn't, his expression hardened. "You know where to find me, honey." He let the door bang behind him.

Christopher stood on the pier, his body stiffly erect as he fished. Wary, Dallas studied the way his white shirt stretched across his shoulders, the way his jeans molded his thighs. The only thing loose about him was the lock of wavy dark hair that fell over his forehead. Every time he cast, his line was like a whiplash flicking the glassy water.

Nervousness tightened her throat, making her wonder how she'd ever find the courage to speak. She licked her lips. "You'll scare them away—casting like that."

He turned. "The way I scare you?" But now there was no anger in his low tone.

She came to him and took his fishing rod. Their hands touched briefly, and so did their eyes with that same acute awareness they always had for each other.

"Do you really think I give a damn about fishing?"

She swallowed and watched him as he unconsciously shook his hair out of his eyes.

"You've got to do it gently." She flicked the line with a delicate motion.

He jammed his fists into his jeans. "It's hard to be gentle when you're impatient as hell."

"If you really want something, you've got to be patient."

"Believe me, I'm trying."

She felt his eyes burning into her as he watched her fish. A few seconds later she reeled in a silvery fish that jumped and flashed on the pier. Smug with triumph, she started to cut it loose, but Christopher knelt down and did it for her.

"You think you're smart," he murmured, amused.

"I live at a marina. I ought to know how to fish. I do know some things besides stuff in books."

When his direct gaze lingered on her hair and lips before meeting her eyes, a sudden tightness gripped her throat.

He said nothing. She shifted uncomfortably.

"And I do thank you for helping me tonight," she added softly.

"It was fun."

"It was," she admitted shyly. "I—I know so little about you."

He was baiting her hook, and she was watching him and thinking he was good with his hands.

"You haven't told me much about yourself, either," he said.

"Because I can't tell anyone."

"Maybe if you tried, the telling would get easier."

"Maybe I don't want it to."

"No, you'd rather writhe in some never-ending purgatory like that shrimp on your hook. You want to feel sorry for yourself forever."

"No! That's not the way it is!" Pleadingly, she looked at him.

"Hey, I've been there, too," he whispered.

She let him take the fishing rod and set it down. Then she was in his arms, burying her face against his chest.

"I can't touch you like I want to," he said. "My hands are all shrimpy."

He was so tough and strong, but his manner with her was infinitely gentle.

"You feel so good, I don't care."

"Honey, I know what it's like to feel so guilty you want to punish yourself forever."

She clung to him for so long that she grew embarrassed. She pulled away, confused. But when he invited her aboard his boat and offered her a beer, she accepted. Together they washed their hands in his sink.

She wasn't used to beer, and soon she felt as if she were floating in a dream. She heard his voice as if from a long way away. "Tell me about the poetry you read."

"You don't really want to talk about Donne and Marvell."

"Right." A pause. "I asked, didn't I?"

The single beer filled her with such a mellow warmth that she forgot the danger of him and began to recite poetry. He liked her poems, and though he hadn't read much poetry, he reinterpreted them for her with masculine irreverence.

"You would never make an English major," she said.

"And that's not all bad."

They laughed together in the hushed silvery darkness. Soon they were talking of their lonelinesses, of their little private hurts. Hours passed in the space of minutes, and neither grew bored. She told him of her family, of loving them and grieving for them. He told her how he'd always longed to feel part of a family and never had. His parents hadn't wanted him. They'd divorced and had rarely bothered to see him after that.

"They should never have had a child," she said.

"There are a lot of people who shouldn't."

She paled.

"You told me you were married," he said. "Were there children?"

She hesitated. Again she was in that white hospital corridor. A single ray of warm sunlight was shining on her baby's golden curls as the baby began to cry. "One. I—I lost her. She had blue eyes and blond hair."

"Like you."

"I only held her once." Her voice trembled.

"It's a terrible thing to lose a child," he murmured, his voice and eyes intense. "Someday you'll marry again."

"No."

He kissed her brow. "There'll be other children."

"No. Please..." She put her fingertips to his lips. "Something went wrong with the pregnancy. I can't have more children. That's one reason why my sister's mean so much."

"I'm sorry."

This time she didn't push him away when he drew her close. His hands stroked her hair again; his whispery voice was reassuring. She nestled against him. She wanted this nearness with him; she had ached for it. *But it was wrong.* She squeezed her eyes tightly shut.

"It was a long time ago," he murmured.

"You carry some things with you all of your life."

"Yes, and you and this night are going to be one of them," he said softly.

The heat in his eyes sent flames through her. At his first tentative touch she grew still.

"What's so special about tonight?" she whispered.

"Until tonight, you've done nothing but run. Tonight you came to me."

His lips touched her hair and moved to her throat, and Dallas trembled at their burning intensity. If only...

She shook her head and cringed away. "I can't."

His grip tightened on her arm. "Why?"

"I can't tell you, either."

"Damn it," he muttered thickly. "Do you have any idea what you're doing to me? Do you even care?"

Passion and jealousy and anger were scrawled across his face. His mouth was set in a bitter line. His fists were clenched. "If I could find the bastard who did this to you, I'd strangle him with my bare hands."

For an instant she couldn't breathe. "It's my fault and no one else's."

He ripped off his glasses. "Tell me! Damn it. Trust me."

Slowly her mute gaze traveled over him. His brown hair was blowing across his brow, and she smoothed it with her fingertips. He grabbed her hand, crushing her fingers inside his. She felt his tension, his power, his strength. His white shirt fluttered against the hard muscles of his dark arms and chest. He exuded raw animal courage, bravery. In so many ways he was her opposite. He was completely wrong for her. But when she looked into his eyes, she knew a terrible truth.

She had begun to love him

"You have your own life. You'll go away," she said.

His eyes narrowed. "I'll take you with me."

She was silent, looking past him. "My life is here," she said at last.

"Life is where your heart is." Lightly his fingers touched her face, tracing the curves of her brows and lashes as if she were very precious to him. "Love me."

Miserable, she shook her head. "The risk just isn't worth it."

His brown eyes surveyed her comprehensively. "It is to me." He grasped her shoulders in his hands. "Let me love you, Dallas. Let me show you that you risk losing more by running." He began to caress her.

But at the touch of his lips and hands, she sprang up wildly. "Excuse me. I feel . . . a little tired."

"Right." Grim understanding glinted in his eyes. Obligingly he let his arms fall to his sides. "I'll see you tomorrow, then?"

She glanced at him in alarm. "No!" Then she shook her head wordlessly.

"Right," he muttered. "We're back where we started— square one. Nowhere."

He didn't try to stop her when she leaped to the dock and raced lightly away.

Nine

Strategy.

It always took strategy to win a war.

Today was Stephie's birthday.

From his yacht, Christopher kept a sharp eye on the kids, especially on Patrick, as the boy stuffed the Jeep with picnic things. Dallas was going to be furious, but, hell, when she'd run away last night, she'd left him no choice.

Why was it that the closer Christopher came to winning her, the harder she fought him? When she had confided in him about the child she had lost, he had felt a new bond. Then she had run again. All day she had avoided him.

The door of her house swung open, and Dallas marched out. Patrick leaned out of the loaded Jeep, stuck two fingers in his mouth and whistled.

At last! Their prearranged signal. Christopher sprang off his boat with his duffel bag and jogged so fast he beat Dallas to the Jeep and opened the door for her.

Stubbornly, she threw her bag on the ground. "Just what do you think you're doing?"

"Excuse me." He pitched his own bag into the Jeep.

"Chance wanted to see Padre Island, so we invited him on my birthday picnic, Aunt Dallas!" Stephie shouted.

"Please, Aunt Dallas!" the older three yelled.

Dallas's gaze went from the kids to him.

"Looks like you're outnumbered, honey," Christopher said.

Dallas bit her lips. "Betrayed."

Christopher's gaze drifted over her. "Sorry you feel that way."

She was wearing a severe black swimsuit that skimmed her body closely, black sandals and a gauzy cover-up. He could see her nipples, the indentation of her navel and much more. Too much more. One glimpse and he was too hot to take another.

"Quit pushing me, Chance."

He smiled at her lazily. "I'm a pushy guy."

"Look, we've got to go."

"Right." He hopped in behind the wheel.

"I'll drive," she said tightly.

"Wrong." He opened the passenger door for her. When she stood by her bag, he started the Jeep.

She stared up at him with blazing eyes. "If you're going, I'm not." She crossed her arms over those delectable nipples and shot him a poisonous look.

"Oh, yes, you are. The kids planned this."

"You're using them."

"Yes." His dark gaze was studying her although she avoided meeting it. He liked what he saw. He would have used the devil himself, to have her. At first he had only wanted Stephie. Now he wanted them all—the whole family. But it was Dallas who was in his blood. Dallas, whose warmth he craved every night when he slept alone in his hard bunk.

"For God's sake," he muttered. "It's Stephie's birthday."

Stephie leaned over from the back seat and threw her arms around Christopher's brown neck. "Chance is the only present I want, Aunt Dallas. If you don't let Chance come, you'll ruin my birthday. And you *have* to come, too. Or we won't be a family."

Great silver rollers of the Gulf of Mexico dashed themselves upon the beach. Patrick and the twins were throwing a Frisbee. Dallas sat stiffly in her lawn chair and pretended to read, but every so often she peeped over the fluttering pages of her paperback and watched Chance and Stephie.

He was marvelous with her. They were building a magnificent sand castle together. "A castle like the princess's," Stephie glowingly had explained to Dallas.

White Horse was propped on a towel near the castle. Stephie dashed about excitedly, scooping up sand, running into the surf and filling buckets with water and then emptying them into their moat. When a bucketful caused a wall to collapse, Chance threw up his hands in mock dismay. Near tears, Stephie grew very still until he beckoned her into his arms.

Dallas smiled as she watched his brown head attentively bend over the little girl's, his fine silky hair blowing about his forehead and hers. He was as lean and bronzed as a pagan prince. Stephie was talking to him so earnestly. He said something, and Stephie's face was transformed by a sweet, shy smile. Soon Stephie's dark eyes were flashing with joy and she was rebuilding the castle.

Chance was so gentle with her. All of the sadness that had haunted Stephie vanished every time she was around him. Funny, she had been terrified of him at first. *Like me,* Dallas thought.

Everyone was having a better time because of him. During the drive when she and Chance had sat stiffly silent, the kids had chattered excitedly because he was there. When Chance had found a deserted place near the dunes for their picnic, the kids would have left her to unpack, if Chance hadn't insisted they help. He had made a game of it, and they hadn't minded.

The castle built, Chance and Stephie joined the Frisbee game. Now, Dallas was the only one left out. She felt odd, watching her family play without her. Suddenly Chance caught the Frisbee. Instead of throwing it to Rennie, he held it until Dallas looked up. When she did, he tipped his head challengingly. She shook her head, hoping that her refusal was very poised, very adult, infinitely superior. His dark eyes danced with defiant mischief, and he threw the disk at her anyway.

She saw everything in slow motion—his wicked grin, the flick of his wrist, the whir of the yellow disk right at her. She screamed. Her paperback sailed into a puddle as she leapt to catch the Frisbee.

She landed on her nose in the sand with her chair on top of her. Everyone laughed as she picked the Frisbee up and slowly stood, dusting herself off.

"Throw it back to him," Stephie screamed excitedly, jumping up and down. "Throw it back."

Dallas ran a shaky hand across her damp forehead. He was watching her. They all were. But she was only aware of him.

He was like a god with the sea breeze blowing his hair, with the sun gleaming on his dark skin. His gaze narrowed on her face and figure, his eyes seeming to physically touch each part of her. He drew his head back, the angle faintly mocking.

She was aware of the pulse beating wildly along her neck, and she knew she was every bit as excited as Stephie.

Then he smiled at her—sheepishly, charmingly, daring her to admit she, too, was glad he'd come. But that she ever would, even though she felt such a sudden rush of sheer joy, her own lips twitched traitorously.

"Catch this if you can," she shouted. Defiantly, she threw the Frisbee just out of his reach. Quicker than lightning, he jumped and caught it, his cocky glance filled with male triumph. Then he tossed it to Rennie, but Dallas had joined the game.

Once, Dallas and Chance both ran after the Frisbee. When she was about to catch it, he caught her and lifted her and spun her around and around until she forgot herself and she shrieked giddily. Her hair whirled loose like a golden cloud. She was flying. She was free and young like a child.

Slowly he let her down so that her soft body slid the muscled length of his. She felt hot and trembly.

She wasn't a child. Neither was he.

His eyes touched her mouth with a suggestive look that sent feverish color flooding up her neck. She gasped. Quickly she stepped back, sucking in air, smoothing her hair, straightening the thin black strap of her swimsuit that had fallen, not daring to look at him, although she was conscious of his hot dark eyes watching her.

The kids grew quiet. There were raised eyebrows, knowing glances between the girls. A red-cheeked Patrick averted his eyes and dug a hole in the sand with his naked toe.

"Hey, you guys," Chance cried, picking up the Frisbee. "Whoever catches this gets a dollar." He sent it flying down the beach, and all four kids went racing after it.

The tension was broken; everyone resumed playing until they were breathless and exhausted and begging Chance to stop.

"I'm hungry," Patrick said, throwing the Frisbee toward the card table set up near the Jeep.

The children dashed toward the table.

Chance turned to Dallas. "I'm hungry, too."

The kids were hidden by the dunes. When Dallas realized she was alone with him on that windswept beach, her heart beat faster. "Why don't we eat, then?" she whispered.

He swaggered nearer. "You tell me."

The laughing glint had left his brown eyes. Something elemental seemed to hover in the air. When he reached for her hand, she let his warm fingers entwine with hers. He led her over to the table.

Patrick swallowed a bite of his hamburger, looked up at them and beamed. Out of the blue he announced, "We used to do this with Mom and Dad. It's almost like we're a real family again."

Chance lifted his head. The warmth in his eyes made Dallas feel slightly dazed. Having Chance with them did make it feel like being in a family, and she was more attracted to him than she had been to anyone.

When they finished eating, Chance said, "Kids, would you mind cleaning up and packing the Jeep?"

"Aw!" Patrick looked disgusted. "We just got here. Do we have to go?"

"Not till your aunt and I get back from our walk."

The kids became instantly quiet, their bright eyes darting speculatively from Chance to Dallas. A significant, grown-up look passed between them. Stephie clutched White Horse shyly.

Jennie was about to object that it wasn't her turn to clear the table, but Rennie silenced her with a sisterly kick.

"Ouch!"

A hush fell upon the table. Rennie rolled her eyes innocently. "Sure, Chance, we'd all just love to clear up."

"Walk as long as you like," Patrick said, encouragingly.

"Till it gets dark," Rennie said, winking at her scowling twin.

Stephie rushed up to Dallas and whispered into her ear. "Please don't say any more mean things to Chance."

When Dallas glanced up at Chance, his inscrutable brown eyes met her wavering look. There was such an aura of male sensuality about him. Her nerves leapt erratically. "You've certainly won over the kids."

His hand closed over her wrist, and she felt her heartbeat flutter. He twisted her around to face him. "Good. That only leaves you."

Every bone in her body seemed to melt. The seascape became a wonderland filled with magic as hand in hand, he led her into the darkening twilight. When they were out of sight of the Jeep, she let him fold her into his arms.

"You've won me, too," she admitted breathlessly as he arched her roughly against his hard body and kissed her.

He ended the kiss. Their lips parted slowly, reluctantly. Then he picked her up and whirled her as he had done when they'd chased the Frisbee. Only this time there was moonlight in her hair, and there were no children watching.

They fell down laughing together in the wet sand. A velvet black canopy sprinkled with sparkling stars enveloped them. A dark wave glimmering with white light dashed over them.

Their laughter died.

The whisper of the waves and wind held erotic promise.

He bent his head to nuzzle her damp hair, and his breath sent shivers of excitement through her.

"I've lain awake every night—wanting this." His hand caressed her breast, his callused fingers molding themselves to the shape of it, kneading her nipple until it crested and her blood flowed in her arteries like hot lava. His fingertips grazed her mouth, tracing its voluptuous fullness until she opened her lips and suckled his fingertips provocatively like a wanton, wanting all of him.

His breathing grew ragged. The moonlight streamed across his face. His gaze was intense and smoldering, his full lower lip half parted with desire. He seemed different tonight, fiercer . . . hungrier.

She moaned sensuously. He gripped her arms so tightly he hurt her, his body pressing into hers. There was only darkness as more warm waves slid over them, only darkness as his lips burned across her skin, burned through the thin layer of her suit, touching her everywhere. He was muttering things she could not understand, his mouth and hands evoking feelings she'd never felt, and she was lost in that sea of swirling sensations and unaware of time or her surroundings. With her eyes tightly shut, she surrendered shudderingly to the abandoned desires of her body. Then salty foam crashed over them, and he pulled her up so they wouldn't both drown in the tidal surge. Another wave followed the first, and they began to laugh. He started to kiss her again.

She touched his lips with her fingertip. "We can't," she whispered. "The children are waiting."

He stopped kissing her and smiled. "Later... then..."

She clung to him, her body still burning where his hands and lips had touched her. "After we put them to bed."

He lifted her from the soft sand and carried her into the surf. Then they dived beneath the waves.

He held her once more as passionately as before, their wet bodies touching and growing hot again. Her arms wound around his neck and her lips trembled beneath his. She pulled him to her tightly.

"Later," he whispered, teasing her.

Laughing, she chased him all the way back to the Jeep.

Sand crabs skittered in front of the Jeep's bobbing headlights, and occasionally there was a fatal pop under the tires. Christopher was oblivious to the scurrying crabs, oblivious to the white dazzling moonlight on the sand and waves. Oblivious, too, to the damp cool sea breeze whirling into the Jeep. All he felt was the warmth of Dallas's slight fingertips he held pressed against his molten thigh.

He could smell her. He could still taste her.

Later.

Rock music throbbed on the radio, and his heart pounded as violently as the wild music. He bit his lips so that he would taste his blood instead of her. But it didn't work. He kept remembering the way she'd felt beneath him in the waves—warm and yielding, shuddering every time he touched her. Every jolt of the Jeep was a fresh stab of fire in his loins.

The white beach stretched before him, as endless as the roaring waves, as endless as the night. He drew a harsh, ragged breath.

He gripped the wheel and bit his lips again, but not even the sharp metallic flavor of his own blood could make him forget the fierce, hot longing.

He wanted her too much. She'd made him wait too long.

Christopher's heart sank when Dallas alighted from the Jeep and teased, "Would you hose the Jeep off, please?" When he scowled, she handed him the hose and sent the children inside to take showers.

He took her wrist and kissed the ardent heartbeat pulsing there. "This is torture. I can't wait," he muttered.

"You'll have to," she whispered gaily. "The Jeep will rust if we don't wash it."

"We?"

"I like you this way—mad for me," she said, touching his lips with the tips of her fingers.

When he tried to press her to him, she jumped away.

"Minx!"

Her teasing eyes flashed playfully, but she had her way. Christopher and the kids unloaded and washed the Jeep while Dallas put things away in the kitchen. Each kid had to shower and dress for bed. They ran out of hot water and a fight erupted between the kids. Christopher attacked his own chores ferociously to dull the edge of his need.

It didn't work.

The minute he saw Dallas's golden hair gleaming in the lamplight while she read huskily to the children, he felt driven to the brink of madness. He had to coil his hands into fists to keep from reaching out and touching her. Finally he went to his boat and took a cold shower. As always, his radio played rock music.

When he stepped into his main cabin wrapped only in a towel, she was there. Like before, she lowered herself down the companionway. Her yellow hair that was damp from her shower flashed with scintillating lights. So did the golden flecks in her blue eyes. His gaze swiftly went over her body. She was sexier than hell in tight jeans and a clingy pink shirt. Her long-lashed eyes lifted uncertainly to his. At his hungry look, her skin glowed a rose color.

Dear God, she was afraid again. Not again. Not when passion throbbed in every cell of his body.

He had to go slow and easy; he felt wilder than the music—out of control. He went and switched off the radio.

"No, leave it on," she whispered.

He turned it back on, and the jungle beat of the music throbbed with the same wildness pulsing in his blood.

He went to her and brushed his hot lips against her forehead. His fingertips trailed from her shoulders down her bare arms. She began to tremble, but she did not kiss him back. A look of infinite sorrow passed fleetingly over her lovely face.

Something was wrong.

He didn't want to stop, but some shred of willpower enabled him to. With an unsteady hand he tipped her chin back gently and looked into her eyes. He was so wild for her that he felt he was on the verge of splintering into a thousand pieces. He wanted to strip her and pull her, naked, against him.

"What's the matter?" he murmured hoarsely.

That desperate look he hated came into her eyes. For an instant she froze. Then she tried to run.

"No. Not tonight, honey," he rasped. He flung himself in front of her and closed the hatch. Then he placed a muscular brown arm on either side of her and pinned her to the wall.

"Let me go! You don't understand!"

He crushed her against his chest, imprisoning her. "Kiss me," he whispered, his body on fire.

"No." She began to fight, kicking him, trying to slap him.

He caught her flying wrists behind her back. "You've got to trust me," he murmured. "I can't stand this anymore. I lie awake wanting you, aching for you."

"You wouldn't if you knew—"

"I still would."

She closed her eyes. Her lashes were damp with unshed tears. "You don't understand!"

"Give me a chance to try."

She began to fight him again, bending and twisting against him, but he held her fast. He felt her panicked heart hammering madly. When she screamed, he let her go.

"Honey, do you really want to always run from everyone who tries to get close to you?"

"Yes!" Her hands were like claws; one of her nails nicked his cheek. A bright line of blood beaded against his dark skin. She drew back, still at last, and gasped in horror, touching it gently.

"Don't!" He winced. "It stings like hell!"

"Oh, dear." She was heartbroken. "I never meant—"

"It's a scratch," he muttered savagely. "Nothing." A pause. "You've got to tell me what's wrong."

She collapsed against him, gazing up at him with dull, lost eyes. "I'm so sorry."

"I said forget it. Just tell me—"

She went to the bathroom, brought back a damp washcloth and placed it against his cheek. "I can't believe I—"

He touched her hair. "Hey, it's okay."

"Maybe you're right. I'll lose you if I tell you, but I'll lose you if I don't." The distant forlorn quality in her voice filled him with fear.

She turned away as if she were too ashamed for him to even look at her. "I didn't tell this to my husband until after we were married. When I finally did, he left."

"What could be so awful?"

"I gave my baby away!"

"What?"

Her face was as white as frost. "The child I lost wasn't my husband's. I had her when I was seventeen. You see, my parents had died, and, oh, I was miserably lonely. This boy came. Suddenly I felt alive again. I was so mixed-up. I didn't know much about boys or love. I went with him once. It was awful, and I knew that night I'd made a terrible mistake. But I got pregnant. Carrie took care of me until the baby was born, and Robert urged me to give up the baby and I did. But the shame, the tragedy of never being able to have another baby... You see, I was supposed to forget and go on with my life, but I couldn't. You want to know something crazy? I celebrate every one of her birthdays."

"When was she born?"

"September the tenth."

"Oh, honey...." His low tone was infinitely gentle.

"I still dream about her, only she's always a little baby. I'm in the hospital. The nurse is carrying her away."

A single tear had beaded on Dallas's lash. It fell and slid down her cheek. Christopher caught it on his fingertip where it glistened like the saddest jewel.

"This September she'll be thirteen. I wake up sometimes and wonder what she's like, if she's really all right, if her adoptive parents love her as I would have. Chance, it's like a part of me is missing."

He knew too well. "Why don't you try to find her?"

"I wish she would look for me someday, but I could never look for her."

"Why not?"

"Because I made all the choices. She has the right to make hers. I don't want to disrupt her life, to risk harming her in any way. She has another family now."

"Why not a letter then—to the adoption agency?"

"I did write, but I never heard anything."

"Don't give up. It's only natural for adoptive parents to be threatened by the biological parent." His grim voice dropped to a whisper. "Maybe someday."

"You see why I gave up everything to take care of my sister's children. When I lost my own parents, I made terrible mistakes. I couldn't let that happen to them."

He held her for a long time. He knew what it was like to lose a child, to death and to adoption, but he had mixed feelings about a woman giving up her baby. Marguerite had given Stephie away. His own mother had all but abandoned him for her career and a succession of husbands and boyfriends.

But the longer he held Dallas, the more he came to realize that what Dallas had done wasn't the same. She'd been a child herself, completely unable to care for a baby. The father had been a boy. She'd acted in the best interests of her child.

"So this guy went away and left you pregnant," Christopher said.

"No. I left him. He would have married me, but my child came first—her life was everything. He didn't love me, and I was too mixed-up to love anybody. We would have had to live with his parents. I would have had security for a while and my child, but we couldn't have had a real marriage. We were both too immature to make it work. I wanted my child to be part of a real family. He finally agreed."

Christopher thought of all the mistakes he had made in his own life—his rebelliousness, Marguerite, Sally and his self-destructive craziness after her death. How could he judge Dallas?

Softly he began to kiss her. "I'm glad you told me. I've done worse," he confessed in a bleak vague tone.

"Maybe someday you'll tell me."

"Not tonight," she whispered, wrapping his arms around her and scooping her onto the bunk.

"Then we'll have no more secrets," she said.

No more lies.

He wanted that even as he wondered if they could survive it. He clung to her, his arms tight and hard around her, determined to have her this once even if it cost him everything. He began to kiss her, his mind spinning deeper and deeper into the eye of a wild passionate whirlwind.

She was as breathless as he when she reached up and took off his wire-rimmed glassed.

He felt naked and exposed as she studied his face. He tried to look away, but she held him still and traced the male beauty of his chiseled features with her fingertips. "You're so handsome—just like a movie star."

He recoiled.

She withdrew her hand and pecked him gently on the tip of nose. "Not that I want you to be a movie star. I want you to be ordinary—just like me. A rancher . . . who can't sail."

"Honey . . ."

Her mouth closed hungrily over his, and his world began to spin again. Her tongue touched his wantonly, and whatever foolish confession he might have uttered was carried away in the flaming whirlwind of his passion.

He wanted her. Tonight. He had to explore the mysteries of her satiny skin, of her long limbs, of her golden hair. His mouth drifted from her lips, down the delicate line of her jaw, her warm neck, to the hollow between her breasts and then to her navel. As sensuously as a cat, she arched herself up, welcoming his lips.

He tore off his towel and straddled her. She gasped with delight and ran her fingers over his shoulders and his chest and down to his waist, lingering over sinewy muscles, and threading her fingertips in the springy hair that covered his chest. Her touching was filled with a breathless urgency that drove him so crazy he would have shredded the pink shirt, if she hadn't ripped it off herself along with her jeans.

At the sight of her body, so pale, so sweetly voluptuous, the wild hunger to have her grew more acute. He pulled her beneath him with a tigerish ferocity and bathed her with his tongue. Then he moved, sinking deeply into her velvet warmth and made her his.

She was perfect. Astonishingly so. Sensations and emotions beyond anything he had ever known consumed him. She made him whole. In the final fiery explosion of ecstasy, he knew that he wanted her forever.

Afterward, he opened the hatch, so that the sea breeze would drift across their perspiring bodies. Beneath the stars they lay in a languorous tangle of coiled limbs, savoring this gentle satiated touching as much as they'd revelled in the wildness. He liked the way her foot lay trustingly on the top of his, the way her head furrowed against his wide chest, and he felt a sweetness, a closeness to her he'd never known before.

They rested in that state of wanton bliss until dawn. Then she got up and kissed him endlessly—until he was so aroused he couldn't bear to let her go.

The sky was aflame when she tiptoed through the dewy grasses back to her house.

Never had he felt so alone. What had happened to him? It was as if he were incomplete without her and couldn't bear to be parted from her—even for a few hours.

No more lies.

He had to tell her.

His eyes felt scratchy and red from wearing his contact lenses so long. He took them off and lay back down alone.

How in the hell could he ever explain?

Ten

Dallas slept until golden sunlight streamed into her bedroom. Bathed in that warm glorious flood, she lay in her bed after she awoke, smiling radiantly as she remembered dreams of wonderlands and paradises shared with Chance. In one he had worn dazzling white-and-silver buckles. He had ridden a white horse like Stephie's knight. How he would laugh if she told him she had dreamed he was her white knight.

She stirred. Just thinking of him made her skin flame. She threw off her sheets and let the light caress her. The bedrolls were empty. The children had gotten up hours ago. Thank goodness. She couldn't have faced them. Not when she felt so soft, so vulnerable. Not with the warm pleasant scent of him clinging to her skin. Stretching, she remembered the delicious passion of the night before, and then the sweet aftermath when Chance had held her for hours.

It seemed to her that ever since her parents had died, she had craved love. At last she had found it.

Not that Chance had actually spoken the words, but he hadn't had to for her to know what he felt. Chance accepted that she had given up her daughter. Dallas laughed at her former doubts. It was all too wonderful to be true.

She got up and showered, moving with a languorous, remote, unfocusing air as she dressed and readied herself to face the children. Once she wrote the name, *Mrs. Chance McCall,* on her steamy mirror, and then quickly rubbed it out, thinking herself silly and young.

This morning she wore shorts that showed her legs, and a blue shirt that clung to her breasts. Into her hair she wound a matching blue ribbon that brought out the color of her sparkling eyes.

When she found Patrick watching *Tiger Four* downstairs, she sank dreamily beside him on the couch. He wasn't supposed to be watching an R-rated movie, but she was too happy to reprimand him. Not even the sight of Christopher Stone masked as *The Tiger* bothered her as much as usual. Vaguely, she wondered why he had stopped pestering her.

She scarcely watched him on a conscious level, but on some other level she did. A lock of his short golden hair stirred across his brow like silk in the wind, and he shook his head the way Chance did sometimes.

The way Chance did sometimes...

She leaned forward to the very edge of her chair. Did she only imagine a resemblance? Her gaze narrowed. *The Tiger*'s mask concealed his features except for his mouth that was exactly like...

Exactly.

Every muscle in her body tensed. She remembered Chance recoiling when she had removed his glasses and said he looked like a movie star.

The mouth, the smile, the jaw—were the same.

But *The Tiger*'s eyes were blue.

Contact lenses! Glasses! No wonder Chance was always taking off his glasses. He could see better without them.

The Tiger's hair was sort and blond.

Chance had let it grow and had dyed it.

She began to tremble. Her heart that had been soft with love hardened with hate. Just as quickly, the hate was washed away by a tide of soul-numbing sorrow. The man she had come to love had used her.

The Tiger spoke, and her heart fluttered at that familiar raspy tone. Whatever lingering doubt she had, dissolved. From the first she had sensed there was something wrong with his accent. He had said he hadn't been born in Texas.

Fool. With a cry she flung herself from the couch.

Patrick looked up as she fled. "Hey, don't worry, the *Tiger* always wins. Watch how he outsmarts Rhydor. This is my favorite part."

She stood at the door, paralyzed, until the movie ended, and letters that spelled *Christopher Stone,* blazed across the screen.

She went into the kitchen and brewed a pot of coffee. If she was a fool, he was a monster. He had let his own child die, and now he wanted Stephie.

Dear Lord.

Patrick came into the kitchen and grabbed a cola from the refrigerator.

"Put that back. You can have orange juice or milk," she said flatly.

His lip curled. But one look at her, and he minded. He splashed orange juice into a glass. "Isn't the *Tiger* the best?"

"The very best," she whispered. *The best lying bastard there ever was.*

She took Patrick into her arms. "Why don't you skate-board or something? I—I don't feel too well."

When he nodded and let her hold him, she was deeply touched. He never used to let anyone hug him. Not until Chance had come. Chance had brought the boy out of his shell.

When Patrick left, she covered her face with her hands. What was happening to them? Because of Chance, Patrick had learned to reach out to people; he had quit lying. Stephie was less afraid, the twins less defiant. By not realizing who he was, Dallas had allowed him to cleverly thread himself into all their lives. She had awakened this morning feeling loved and cherished. Now she felt shattered. Christopher had used her; he had cruelly deceived all of them—to get Stephie.

Dallas's disillusionment was profound. There was no way she could believe that a movie star could possibly be interested in her. Once again she had made a terrible mistake with a relationship. Only this time she had involved four children. She couldn't believe he cared for them at all.

Dallas went to the window and lifted the curtain. Christopher was moving about on his boat. For a dizzy moment she remembered the blazing thrill of his expert lovemaking. How he must be laughing at her. She thought of how she'd clung to him for the whole night. She was ashamed of the way she had revelled in what his hands and mouth had done to her. Now she felt herself brought low by every kiss, every torrid moan. He hadn't had to force her. She had wanted him too desperately. No doubt he'd considered her no more than a delightful diversion to be enjoyed while he claimed his daughter. He probably even despised her a little. He had a reputation for treating women callously. Was he planning to accuse her of being unfit to be Stephie's mother because she had slept with him? The coffee on her empty stomach made Dallas feel nauseous, and she pitched a cupful into the sink.

Last night she had nearly wept at the sight of blood on Chance's cheek. She looked down at her nails and longed to claw him like a cat.

No. She doubled her hands so that the nails were concealed. The curtain fell back into place. She began to wash dishes. Her hands trembled, and she broke a glass. She cut her finger on a gleaming shard and watched her blood flow onto the white porcelain.

No, she wouldn't go to him. She would stay in the house and compose herself. She would wait until he came for her. Then she would be as clever as he and show him that he was not the only one who could be deceitful.

Dallas had been careful never to be alone that morning. When she heard Christopher on the porch, she clutched Stephie tightly, shrinking behind her as if she were a shield.

When Dallas saw his tall figure through the screen, a mixture of confused emotions coursed through her. He hesitated a moment as if he, too, found it difficult to face her. Then restlessly he pulled the door open.

His face was dark with telltale guilt. He tried to smile, and she sensed the uneasy tension in him that he was fighting to conceal.

She was just as nervous. Her cheeks flamed. Her brow was damply perspiring. She clasped her hands together so he wouldn't notice she was shaking.

He saw.

Unaware of the terrible adult tensions in the room, Stephie flipped the page of her storybook and commanded, "Read."

The deep timbre of Christopher's anxious voice filled the kitchen. "What are you girls reading—the white knight story?"

"No, Chance!" Stephie cried. "It's about a wolf that comes to the house of some goats and they let him in when they're not 'sposed to. And he eats 'em all."

That about summed it up. Dallas stared straight at an illustration of the unlucky goats.

For an instant Christopher didn't speak. "Honey, are you sure you should be reading her such grisly stuff?"

"I think it's a good preparation for life."

His mouth tightened with disapproval.

"I like it," Stephie chimed.

"Well, I don't." He leaned down and snapped the book shut. "You run out and play," he commanded briskly. At Stephie's startled look, his manner became gentle. "I want to talk to your aunt."

As soon as the child was gone, he took Dallas into his arms. "What's wrong now?" He was staring at her white face and frowning as if he was genuinely concerned. "Honey..."

The endearment was so tender, so anxious, so perfect. A muscle in her stomach pulled. Oh, he was good. So good. And he felt good, too. *He was a monster.* But her heart began to race absurdly. Why couldn't she be immune to being crushed against the hardness of his virile chest?

She felt on the edge of hysteria. Her mouth was too dry for her to speak; her eyes misted. She turned away so he wouldn't see.

But he saw. He took a quick breath. "Don't cry, Dallas." A pause. His fingers stroked her neck with expert gentleness. "I can't stand it when you cry." He kissed her brow.

When she felt her own treacherous response to the comfort of those lips, she jumped away. "Don't. Not now. The children might come in." She bit her lips and wondered how he found it so easy to lie when it was killing her.

"All right." His voice held a faint note of exasperation. "If you're sure it's just the kids."

"I'm sure." She drew a deep breath and sighed.

"We've got to tell them about us sometime."

"No!" she snapped, terrified.

The question in his fake brown eyes seared her.

Careful.

In a calmer voice, she continued, "Of course, we will, but not today. There won't be enough time to explain. I—I have to take the kids into town."

"I'll come with you."

She rushed to the window. "No—"

His dark watchful gaze followed her. "I've never seen you like this before."

She whirled. "Like what?"

"So nervous. If it's guilt about last night—"

Oh, you should be an expert on guilt. For an instant her eyes blazed. "Oh, it's not guilt!"

"Then what is it?"

She lowered her gaze. "Maybe I wasn't sure what you'd think of me."

"I'm crazy about you," he said ardently, going to her and drawing her into his arms.

His face was very still. His hot dark eyes lit a fire inside her, and her heart began to beat wildly. He was lying. He was manipulating her with soft looks and sweet words, and she was so starved for love, she almost believed him.

"You can't come because I'm taking them to my brother's," she said softly, shakily.

"I see," he said in a level voice.

"No, you don't." She forced herself to touch his hand, to smile at him, and her heart twisted at how these tendernesses from her softened his hard features.

He lifted aside the molten gold of her long hair, pushing it away from the base of her throat so his lips could brush the vulnerable heartbeat there. She gasped when he kissed her in such a charming, loverlike way. Then she told herself not to be a fool. He was an actor.

In a rush she began again. "I'm going to leave them there all night, so that you and I can be alone."

His arms tightened around her waist, and he molded her closer. The hunger in his fathomless eyes made the muscles of her stomach contract sharply.

"We'll have the whole night, Chance. Just us."

"I can't wait." He bent his head and kissed her ear. Desire licked through her at the darting probes of his wet tongue. "Have you ever made love in the morning?"

"Chance, no! I—I mean we can't this morning." A pause. More softly. "But tonight I'll show you just how much last night meant to me."

His low voice was husky. "I'm looking forward to it." He forced himself to let her go.

She turned away. "Oh, so am I."

But she wasn't.

Not at all.

The heat of the day was dying, and the violet sky was streaked with mauve when Dallas came back from the city. She stopped at home, packed the Jeep with wine, food, the twins' boom box, towels and a blanket before continuing on to pick up Chance.

"Where are we going?" he murmured, kissing her after he climbed into the vehicle.

One kiss and she was melting and clinging to him, surrender quivering through every female cell. "The beach again," she managed shakily, pulling away reluctantly.

"I'd better go back for my suit," he said.

"Oh, you won't need it." With no effort she made her voice light and breathless as if in husky anticipation. She ran her fingertips along his muscular arm, and a mixture of dread and excitement tingled through her.

At his sudden groan she yanked her hand away. His dark smoldering gaze focused on her, and she felt the magnetic power of his charm. Her cheeks burned. He started to say something, but she couldn't bear to listen to more of his lies. Quickly she turned on the radio so she wouldn't have to.

But his silence was almost worse than his talking would have been. He watched everything she did with an intensity that made her nervous. He was so keenly intuitive, she wondered if he suspected something.

She was too aware of his virile silent presence beside her. Nor could she stop the tantalizing memories of the night before. Every time she looked at him she remembered the way they'd lain in the sand with the surf curling over them, the way they'd driven for miles afterward with the wanting fierce between them. And all the rest came back, as well.

When she came to the turnoff to the beach, he placed his hand on her thigh and ignited a heat that shamed her. She stepped on the gas so that the Jeep made the turn on two tires.

"Sorry," she said curtly when he was thrown against his door.

A white grin flashed across his tanned features. "Easy. We have the whole night."

She forced a smile even as her heart filled with dread. She drove even faster than before.

A big yellow moon rose over the gulf. The rhythm of the music was a savage beat pulsing through her blood.

"Can't we stop?" he murmured after they'd sped past several likely looking spots.

The Jeep whirled past still another spot in a rush of throbbing rock music and flying sand. "No!"

His dark gaze scanned her features, his own expression inscrutable. Her nervous fingers curled around his hand. "I—I want to go farther than we went last night," she murmured on a boldly breathless note.

"I'm up to whatever you are."

The miles whirred past them in a blur of sparkling waves until they had gone so far there were no other cars. The beach road grew rougher. The gulf had washed it out in places, and she had to drive through shallow water.

"Aren't you afraid of getting rust under your Jeep?" he asked.

"It'll be worth it."

The cool damp sea breeze caressed her. The wild music aroused her. The longer she drove, the more she craved him. But she drove thirty miles down the beach before she took a deep breath for courage and braked. Her fingers flew to her car keys and then froze. *She'd better leave them there.*

It was a beautiful night. The moon washed water and sand with gold. Endless beach and glimmering waves surrounded them. It seemed to her that they were the only two people in the world. Her heartbeats echoed in a wild, deafening roar that blanked out the surge of the surf. She glanced toward him. He seemed relaxed, seemed to suspect nothing. His hand moved to her shoulder and eased her spaghetti strap lower. She laid her head back so that his mouth could explore her shoulder, and he pressed a kiss against the curve of her neck.

As his expert mouth moved across her bare skin she was filled with that strange combination of fear and exhilaration. His large warm hands began to roam and skillfully mold. Everything he did aroused a warm flood of exquisite sensations that terrified her.

At last his lips covered her mouth in a long, drugging kiss. The kiss was like a narcotic, weakening her will and relaxing her rigid muscles. She could feel her heart thumping against her ribs. Her arms slid limply around his neck. She didn't want to desire him, but some strong primeval instinct overpowered all her will to resist.

If she didn't act quickly, she wouldn't be able to. She slid free of his embrace. "Let's swim."

"I'd rather spread the blanket on the sand," he murmured.

Her heart fluttered wildly. "Not yet." She touched his hot cheek with her palm. "Why don't we work up an appetite first?"

"Honey, I'm already starving."

Dallas looked up at him from beneath sweeping eyelashes. "I want to hold you in the water," she whispered. "To feel the waves curl around our hot bodies. It's a fantasy of mine."

As she began to pull off her shirt, he took a deep controlling breath and hesitated for a second only. Then gently, carefully, he helped her. She tossed her shirt into the back seat. Her fingertips hesitated at the clasp of her bra. He tore off his own shirt and threw it carelessly on top of hers.

His dark naked torso gleamed. Dallas's pulse fluctuated in alarm at so much rippling muscle. He looked strong and powerful, like some primitive noble savage. She thought of what she was about to do to him, and some inner vice warned that there might be danger in pushing a man like him too far.

His hungry dark eyes watched her unfasten her bra. That, too, she removed. Quickly he unlaced his boat shoes while she untied her sandals. These were quickly tossed to the back. Then she undid the waistband of her shorts. He watched her peel yellow cotton and silky panties down over her thighs. Nervously she pulled them lower. His possessive gaze blazed a fiery path over her nude body. With a stifled groan, he finished undressing.

She was just as affected by the sight of him. He was beautiful. Lean sinewy muscle gleamed. He was virile, all-male—dangerous. But his expression was tender.

She loved him. More than anything she wanted to know again the ecstasy of his lovemaking. She continued to look at him, her emotions and thoughts tearing at her. Maybe... she was wrong about him.

No. He had made a fool of her.

"Honey, what is it?"

Her mouth went dry. She drew a deep breath. "Oh, nothing." Self-consciously, guiltily, she averted her eyes.

"Don't be afraid," he whispered gently.

"I'm not," she managed in a softer voice, but when he tried to touch her reassuringly, she bolted.

He ran after her, catching her at the water's edge and pulling her down into the foaming waves. The water was cool, but his mouth was warm, and she was as dangerously vulnerable to his lovemaking as ever. Every kiss sent passionate shivers racing down her spine. She was on the brink of total surrender, when he murmured, "How about that blanket now?"

Numbly she nodded.

His mouth crooked, utterly charming her. Once more he kissed her. Then he left her and swam out into the surf to wash himself off.

For a second longer, she watched him, no longer wanting to trick him, even as she despised herself for hesitating. It was now or never. This was not the time for second thoughts. When he turned around, she was already racing toward the Jeep. He called out, but she only ran faster.

Shells cut into her bare feet, and she cried out in pain. But his footsteps thudding behind her kept her running.

Breathless, she threw herself into the Jeep. She turned the keys in the ignition. Jammed her foot on the accelerator.

Nothing happened!

He loomed nearer. The surf roared. All she heard was his harsh panting. She twisted the key again. All she felt were the thuds of his running feet hitting the sand.

Frantically she twisted the key a final time.

He grabbed the door handle. "What the hell do you think you're doing?"

The engine sputtered to life.

He banged on the window as the Jeep inched away. "Dallas!"

She looked into the wild fury of his eyes and stepped on the gas. He fell back as the Jeep shot forward.

She heard his furious shouts and stopped a safe distance from him, rolling her window down and leaning out. "Nice night. As they say in California—enjoy... *Mr. Stone.*"

"Dallas! Wait! I can explain!"

"No!"

"You can't leave me like this—without money or clothes."

"Right!" She threw out a towel. "That's more than you deserve."

"Dallas!"

She stomped on the accelerator. Tires spun sand all over the towel.

A mile or so down the road she stopped—to put on her clothes.

Eleven

Through the salt spray on the windshield Dallas saw the blur of her house and the restaurant beside it.

Go back and get him.

Her teeth sank viciously into her bottom lip. She jerked the wheel, accelerated and swerved onto the shell drive. Then she leapt out without bothering to unpack and went straight to the restaurant to work. If Oscar and Pepper knew something was wrong, they asked no questions.

It was late when Dallas unplugged the jukebox and locked up after the last customer. In her bedroom she collapsed without bothering to turn out the lights. In a state of sleepless exhaustion, she lay fully clothed, staring up at those burning lights.

A thousand times she was tempted to drive back for Chance. A thousand times she stopped herself. What she had done was nothing compared to what he had done to her.

But at first light, she went to his boat almost hoping he was there.

He wasn't.

The yacht strained gently against her dock lines when Dallas pulled on them. She had so many questions. Perhaps she could find answers here. Warily she slid his hatch open and eased herself into the darkened cabin.

Inside one drawer she found the script for *Tiger Six*. She pitched it back on top of several others. Inside another drawer she discovered his clothes, or rather his costumes—Western shirts, jeans, enormous belt buckles. Angrily she slammed that drawer shut on a tangle of jeans and belts. In the last she found a large envelope stuffed with photographs of herself and her family plus type-written reports about her. There were letters from his lawyer that made Christopher's intentions damningly clear. A chill went through her as she read the documents.

Her eyes burned. With shaking hands she threw everything back into the drawer. There was no doubt that what he had planned all along was to take Stephie. As always, Dallas had been so eager to find love that she had blindly slept with the one man who wanted to use her. She had seen only what she wanted to see, believed what she'd wanted to believe.

With a leaden heart she returned to the house and called Robert, saying only that she'd be late picking up the children. He argued even after she told him it was an emergency. Then he started asking her about Chance.

"Not now."

"The kids can't quit talking about him. He sounds great."

"Maybe to you."

"The kids are anxious to go home. I could drive—"

"No! I—I mean not just yet."

"I want to meet this guy."

"No!"

"Dallas—"

She hung up on him.

No way did she want the children and Robert around when she had it out with Christopher.

The morning dragged on and on, and despite her anger and her fear of Christopher, she began to worry that something terrible had happened to him. So it was with a curious mixture of dread and relief that she watched a battered blue pickup unload him at the marina.

Christopher climbed out, exhaustion in every stiff muscle of his body. He cringed with every bleeding step he took across the rough drive, clutching his towel about him.

Not that she believed he was beaten. She braced herself for him to come to the house at once.

But he didn't.

The longest hour of her life passed. She chewed her lips until they were raw.

Finally she couldn't stand the suspense and went down to him. From a distance he appeared to be dozing nonchalantly on his cushions in the shade of his bimini. At her footsteps, his eyelids flickered alertly open. His hair was still long and brown, but his famous eyes were a piercing blue.

The Tiger's eyes.

He went as still as death when he saw her. Although her heart began to pound, she was determined not to show her fear. He got up and leaned over to pull the dock line tight so she could step on board.

Christopher said nothing. Finally she burst out, "Quit looking at me like that!"

"Like what?"

"Like I should feel guilty."

"And do you feel guilty?" His cold blue gaze was intense.

"That sounds like something a crazy actor who's spent too much time on an analyst's couch would ask."

"I've never been to a shrink."

She flushed. "You know you had it coming."

His mouth tightened. "Right. You would think that."

"I'm not the guilty one here."

His face took on a cold seductive expression that attracted her even as it repelled her. "Right. I'm the bastard. You're the angel. Black and white. Maybe your life's that simple, *angel.*"

She raked her fingers through her blowing hair and looked away. There were smudges of blood on the floor of the cockpit—from his feet. She imagined the long walk over shells and sand and the occasional bits of broken glass. She saw the dark shadows under his eyes.

"Angel!" He said the word viciously. "The last thing I expect from you is kindness."

"Don't worry! I—I don't feel any. You're worse even than all those newspapers said you were!"

Christopher kept looking at her with those icy blue eyes. "Then I won't bother defending myself. Narrow-minded people always believe what they want, no matter what the truth is."

"Quit trying to make me into the bad guy."

"You're the one who refused to let me even see my child. You left me thirty miles down the beach without shoes or a stitch of clothes while you went home and slept like a baby. You went through my things."

"You used me," she accused.

He slumped back against the cushions. "Because you were so set against me you wouldn't even listen to me."

"I knew you'd lie."

"I had no choice." His face was as bloodless as a statue's. "I had no choice."

"Why did you make love to me?" Tears began to stream down her cheeks. "Maybe I could have forgiven you the rest, if only it weren't for that." She buried her head in her hands because she couldn't bear for him to see her cry.

"I'm not proud of what I did."

Dallas flushed miserably. "That makes two of us."

"If I could undo it, I would."

"Ditto."

"But I couldn't get anywhere with Robert. He kept demanding more money for Stephie. Every time I agreed, he wanted more. When I tried dealing with you, I got nowhere. I came here to see what was going on."

"You did a little more than that. You won the children's trust and mine. With lies. You pretended you cared."

"I do care."

The passion in his voice sent fresh longing surging through her which made her more ashamed then ever. How could she—*want to believe him?* "It was all a game, an act, a role to you."

"No."

She looked up, her tears gone. "I want you gone."

His icy gaze studied her. "It's not that simple."

She got to her feet. "It is to me. I hate you now."

Just for a second she thought she saw some terrible vulnerability in his eyes that was equal to her own. She had a crazy, odd feeling that she had cut him deeply.

"Be careful that you don't push me too far," he warned, "I didn't lie to you about my feelings. There was nothing false in my kisses."

"No..."

"Nothing false in my lovemaking. I burned for you then . . . as I burn for you now."

Her fingers twisted the bottom edge of her shirt; her nervous palms were moist. "I—I can't believe you," she whispered even as his tender words made her blood race like liquid fire. "I can't—"

"Then believe this, you little fool."

She lunged wildly away, but he was quicker. He seized her, his arms encircling her. Her legs tangled with his rock-hard thighs. His mouth ravaged hers, his tongue roaming possessively inside her mouth.

Every barrier between them vanished in the heat of that destroying kiss. With his hands and mouth, he made her his.

One minute she was spinning in that dark whirlwind of his fiery passion, craving him as undeniably as she craved breath, air, life itself. In the next she clawed him frantically to escape.

He let her go.

She fell back limply against the lifelines. He saw the blood on her lips and, thinking he'd hurt her, touched them gently with his fingertip. She jerked her head away.

"That may work in the movies, but not in real life," she said bitterly. "I wonder if you know the difference."

His dark face paled. "I'm sorry I deceived you."

"Oh, so that makes everything all right."

He clenched his hands into fists. "No. Damn it."

"For once you're right about something!"

In the distance a car door slammed. Neither of them heard the soft eager approach of a little girl's running footsteps. Neither of them saw her stop and crouch low behind a nautical gear box on the deck when she heard their angry voices.

"Dallas, listen to me. Don't be like all the others. You don't know the hell it has been—living a fishbowl existence. Don't judge me on what a sensational press has written. Writers who don't know me make up stuff about what I do, about what I feel. I'm not that person.

"The last few weeks have been the only good, the only real thing in my life for a long, long time. I wasn't pretending that I cared for you and the kids. I was born into this crazy movie-star existence. I can't even begin to tell you how awful it was. My parents lived soap-opera lives and thrived on the publicity. They fought over me in endless custody battles, and when one of them won me, he or she ignored me."

He stopped for a second before continuing.

"Honey, my life has always been like a circus, like some nightmare carnival ride. My marriage to Marguerite was no different. She never wanted me—she wanted Hollywood—

the glamour, the money, not that any of it ever made her happy. None of it has ever made me happy, either. It wasn't real. Only you. You were real, Dallas. The kids were real—not just Stephie, but all of them. Patrick, Rennie, Jennie. For the first time I felt I was part of a real family.''

Dallas had looked away, into dark water when he began speaking, not wanting to hear because she was too afraid she might believe. Tears glimmered in her eyes as every sweet word and every sad one tore into her heart. *Did he have any idea how she longed to believe him and ached because she couldn't?*

"You deserve an Academy Award for that speech," she managed at last, her choked voice like ice.

"Damn it. Dallas, I'm telling you the truth. What would you have done? You had my child!"

Something fell on the dock, and he looked up abruptly. "What was that?"

Dallas glanced toward the dock. "Probably just something the wind knocked over."

"Hell, I lost my train of thought." He ran his hands through his hair.

"I had your child," Dallas reminded him dully.

"Right." A pause. "I couldn't just go away and leave her here. If you'd known who I was, you would have thrown me out the first day. I would never have gotten to know any of you."

"At least I would have known what I was dealing with. A snake." She paused. "I loathe you. You are the vilest human being I've ever known. I don't care if you are Stephie's father. I want you gone."

His face twisted. "If only it were that easy."

"You walked out on her mother seven years ago. Why don't you just do the same thing now?"

"You don't even begin to understand about Marguerite. I was crazy about her, but our relationship was a destructive force in both our lives. I didn't know about the baby when I left her. I damn sure didn't know about it when I came back to her. She was too scared she'd lose me again to tell me the truth. She thought she could forget and go on with her life, but the lie ate at her and destroyed any hope we ever had of an honest relationship. The minute I found out about Stephie I came here."

Dallas's temples pounded sickeningly. "We were doing just fine before you came."

"Oh, right. What about Stephie nearly walking off the dock that first night? What about her being all mixed-up and afraid of everything? I think she's grown attached to me."

"Because she doesn't really know you. You're not who you pretended to be," Dallas said. "I've read awful things about you."

"I wish I could say they were all lies."

"All those women."

"I regret them. I went crazy... after Sally died. Those women didn't mean anything to me."

"I doubt they felt as casually about it as you do."

"It was different with you."

She was looking at him closely, some part of her believing him. He seemed so sincere. Why was it so hard to keep telling herself he was a monster? Why, despite his glamour, did he seem a real human being after all, too real? She remembered the baby she'd given up, the agony of the years wondering about that unborn child. How could she blame him for wanting to find his daughter?

But when he moved toward her to draw her closer, she sprang away, shaking her head. "Don't you dare come near me."

"Okay," he said. "We'll take it slow, if that's the way you want it."

"I don't want anything from you, Mr. Stone."

"I'm not leaving here without what I came for."

There was a small frightened cry from the dock. Then there was nothing.

"What was that?" Christopher demanded.

"It sounded like Stephie."

In a single leap he was off the boat. Behind the gear box they found White Horse thrown down and abandoned.

Robert had brought the kids back anyway.

"Stephie..." Christopher's voice was a whisper.

"She must have heard us."

"Dear God. If anything has happened to her, I'll never forgive myself. I thought you said the kids were at your brother's."

"I—I thought they were."

Christopher knelt down and picked up the grubby white horse. "White Horse was sitting by the pool the day Sally died. He's all I have left of her."

The unbearable anguish in his bleak, frightened voice struck Dallas to the heart. Her anger vanished. Without thinking, she touched his arm and said gently, "Stephie's okay. She's upset. She does this sometimes. We'll find her."

His hand closed over hers tightly. "Right, we'll find her."

"It's not your fault," she murmured.

No matter how she might hate him for what he'd done, he loved Stephie as much as she did. Maybe he had lied to her and used her because of that love. Maybe he was wild and terrible. Maybe she even hated him.

But it was funny how none of that seemed to matter. How the only thing that mattered now was the love they both shared for their lost little girl.

Twelve

Stephie was gone!

Christopher was exhausted—physically, mentally and emotionally. He'd walked nearly all night; it had been dawn before the battered pickup had stopped for him.

Nevertheless, after Dallas and he searched the marina, calling to Stephie and she didn't answer, he ran up to the house and barked out orders to Robert and the children, sending everyone in opposite directions to look for Stephie.

Christopher was the one who found her, though.

Because the first place he looked for her was at the pool. She was lazily floating in the deep end, clinging to a black inner tube.

He strode up to the water's edge. "Stephie, why didn't you answer me when I called you awhile ago?"

She turned her head away.

"You have everyone worried. They've all looking for you."

No answer. Only the tiny movement of her small hand, only the silver wavelet rippling away from her clenched fingertips.

He sucked in a heavy breath. The glassy water was a turquoise dazzle. Stephie's black hair was loosely flowing across the surface as she lay on her back staring up at the sky. When he jumped in, she continued to hold her face away from him.

"Clouds go by so fast," she whispered, closing her eyes when he swam up to her. "Where do you think they're going?"

"Don't you know you shouldn't ever swim alone?"

"I'd like to ride on a cloud."

"I said you shouldn't swim . . .?"

"I've got my tube."

"That doesn't matter, Stephie."

"You're my birth daddy, aren't you?" For the first time she opened her eyes, and her dark eyes seemed to pierce all the way to his soul.

A pause.

"Yes."

"You came here because you want to take me away."

"I wanted to see you. Is that so wrong?"

She looked back to the clouds. "I don't know. Aunt Dallas seems to think so."

"That's because I tricked her. Have you ever done something to a friend you wished you hadn't?" He began to gently pull Stephie and the tube toward the shallow end. "You knew who I was right from the first."

"But I thought you were bad."

They had reached the steps. "What do you think now?"

"Your real little girl died, didn't she?"

"Yes. But you're my real little girl, too."

"Am I the only little girl you have now?"

"The only one."

She let go of the tube and wrapped her arms around his neck. "You're my only daddy, too, and I don't think you're bad. You'll have to tell Aunt Dallas you're sorry."

His forehead touched Stephie's. "I already did. She won't listen."

"She does that to me, too. Sometimes Patrick hits me first, and when I hit him back she just sends us both to our rooms." She frowned. "I like your eyes better now."

"Thank you."

"How did you make them brown?" Before he could answer, her grip around his neck tightened. "Please don't take me away from Aunt Dallas and the kids, okay? 'Cause I love 'em."

"I love them, too."

"Even Aunt Dallas?"

"Especially Aunt Dallas."

"Like the knight loved the princess?"

"Right... Well, not exactly. Honey, I'm afraid there's no such thing as fairy-tale love."

"That's what Aunt Dallas said."

"And I'm not much of a knight, either."

"You are to me."

"Then I'm a tarnished one."

"Guess who Chance really is, everybody," Stephie announced in a happy piping voice as he carried her through the screen door on his shoulders. "He's my birth daddy!"

For one paralyzed second there was a profound silence in the crowded kitchen. Everyone seemed to hold his breath. Only the faint rush of the sea breeze rustling the bushes outside could be heard. All eyes focused on Christopher and Dallas.

Dallas turned beet red.

Everyone started talking at once.

"Christopher Stone," the twins gasped in an awed breathless duet. "Wow! We know a real movie star."

"The Tiger!" Patrick gave an excited war whoop. "I knew it all the time!"

"Liar!" the twins yelled.

"I did!"

Christopher was aware only of Dallas. Every drop of hot color had swiftly drained from her face. She swayed back into Robert's supporting arms a grim, confirming look passing from younger sister to older brother.

Robert was tall and blond, a masterful male version of Dallas. He had the same golden flecks in his blue eyes. He held out his hand to Christopher and introduced himself. His handshake was firm and welcoming. Christopher sensed an ally.

"Last night, when the kids couldn't stop talking about this Chance McCall, I couldn't figure it out," Robert said. "Now it's all beginning to make sense."

"Where was Stephie?" Dallas asked quietly when her brother had finished, concern for the child in her every breath.

"In the swimming pool."

"Dear Lord. Stephie, darling, why didn't you answer when we called?"

"I got scared when you said those mean things to Chance."

Dallas went even whiter at this censure. She turned to the twins. "Rennie ... Jennie ... bring some towels."

Not wanting to miss a second in the kitchen, the twins obeyed instantly, streaking like lightning to the bathroom and back with a bundle of fleecy towels.

Dallas reached for a towel at the same moment Christopher did. Their eyes met. Her fingers tightened just for an instant on her end of towel and then relaxed, letting him pull the soft cotton from her.

Dallas slumped weakly into a chair. Robert began to make coffee. On the surface everyone tried to act calm, and yet Christopher felt tension running through them all.

He leaned over Stephie as he wrapped her in a towel and then took a second one and dried her hair. When he was done, he sat down, and Stephie crawled up into his lap and put her arms around him.

Dallas went still paler at the sight of the little girl clinging lovingly to her father. When the coffee was brewed, Robert poured his sister a steaming black cup. "You look like a ghost. Maybe this'll help."

She gulped it down gratefully, trying not to look at Christopher and Stephie.

Robert was the first to recover. "I think this is for the best," he said in his most lawyerlike voice.

"Robert, please." Dallas set her cup on the counter with a clatter.

"I was only trying to help."

"I wish you wouldn't."

"This doesn't have to be a tug of war," Robert persisted.

"Then what is it?" she demanded through gritted teeth.

"Why don't you face the facts, Dallas? He's her father."

"We've been through this before," she said tightly.

"You're her mother. I told you that last night the kids couldn't stop talking about him. In the few weeks he's been here, they've formed an extraordinary attachment to him. Whether you like it or not, he's earned a place in this family. Besides that, it costs an arm and a leg to raise four kids..."

She jumped up. "Well, I don't like it! It always comes down to money with you, doesn't it? And I can't stand you taking his side in this, either! You're my brother."

"Did it ever occur to you that you might both be on the same side?"

"No!"

"Then maybe it should. I think if you tried, you could work out a compromise that would be fair to everyone. You need his help. The kids need him."

Dallas whirled on Christopher. "You must be very happy."

Gently, Christopher set Stephie down and stood up. "No...."

"You knew exactly what you were doing, and you think you've won. *The Tiger* always wins. They all love you—Robert, the children—all of them, except me. You've torn this family apart with your lies, with your deceit."

"Dallas, stop it." Robert was aghast.

Christopher seemed to steel himself to her cold voice, even to the fury in her eyes. "No. Let her say it. She has to get it out. I did trick her, and what I did was wrong. Even though I did it because I cared about...everybody in this room."

"Liar! Don't listen to him," she whispered. "He's as cold and as inhuman as that...muscle-bound idiot he plays."

"I like *The Tiger,* Aunt Dallas," Patrick dared to say hesitantly.

"We do, too," said the twins, moving closer to Christopher.

"Dear Lord! I can't stand any more. Mr. Stone, tell the children goodbye. Then I want you gone. They'll forget you."

"No, we won't," Patrick said.

"You don't have the right to make this decision for us," Rennie muttered.

"Kids, don't make it harder for her than it already is," Christopher said quietly.

For a second Dallas hesitated and stared at them all with desperate haunted eyes. Then she raced upstairs, stumbling over Patrick's skateboard.

The skateboard rolled down the stairs, crashed into the table and turned over on its side. Patrick's eyes grew huge with guilt when she nearly fell, but no one said a word. The only sound in the kitchen was the soft, dying whir of the skateboard's spinning wheels.

"Wow!" Jennie gasped.

Rennie kicked her, and Jennie looked embarrassed.

Patrick was the next to speak. "I wish you really were *The Tiger,* Chance. 'Cause he always wins."

Christopher swallowed hard as he gravely considered the boy's words. "Hell, I wish I was him, too."

"Go after her anyway, Chance," Patrick urged. "Maybe she just needs a hug."

Christopher sank to his haunches and picked up the skateboard. "That makes two of us."

Patrick came flying across the kitchen into his arms.

Not to be left out, Stephie threw her arms around both of them. Rennie and Jennie giggled nervously, and then joined their brother and sister on the floor.

Christopher hugged them all for a long time, drawing a kind of strength from their love and faith in him that he'd never known before.

Finally he got up, knowing he had to face Dallas.

Robert came over and picked up the skateboard. "This house is a mine field." He handed the skateboard to Patrick. "Why don't you put this away for once? We've got broken hearts already. We don't need a broken neck." To Christopher, he said, "There's only one way to win Dallas— I know because I'm her brother. Don't give up."

Christopher pounded on Dallas's bedroom door for an eternity before she finally answered.

He heard her muted voice, still and small, float across her room. "Oh, if you won't go, come in."

He entered and closed the door.

She was lying on her bed in the shadows, shaking. "When are you leaving?"

"I'm not—without you."

She sat up on her elbows. "You can't stay!"

"No," he agreed. "I've stayed way too long. I've neglected my work, my business associates. My agent even hung up on me the other morning, and that's a dangerous sign in Hollywood. You're coming with me. You and the children. As I see it, there's only one solution."

"That you go!"

"No."

She stared up at him blankly.

"I'm asking you to marry me." With a knightly flourish, he sank onto a bended knee.

She sprang up, her blue eyes burning brightly in a face that was white with horror. "Are you out of your mind? Get up!"

"If you believe everything you read—"

"Be serious. What kind of marriage could we possibly have?"

"It couldn't be worse than any of my parents' marriages or than my first one," he replied bitterly, rising.

"What sort of person says something like that?"

His mouth quirked. "Can I help it if I have only my own experience to speak from? Our marriage would be as good as most of the ones I've known."

"That sounds so cynical."

"As you've pointed out, my life hasn't been ideal."

"Don't you even care about love?"

"I don't know much about love other than what I've read about or seen in the movies. It's a word people slap on to everything to excuse the most stupid, self-destructive behavior."

"I gave up my own child because her father didn't love me. How could you possibly even think I'd consider marrying you without it?"

"This is different. You were a child yourself then." He stopped. "We're already a family."

"No."

"We're two responsible adults."

"That's debatable."

"Damn it, Dallas. Six lives hang in the balance. If you marry me, we all win."

"Wrong. We all lose."

"We'd be together."

"For how long? You only want this because you want your daughter. These kids have already lost their mother and father once. I won't risk a divorce that would shatter their lives all over again. You'd try to take Stephie then. If I marry you, that will strengthen your claim to her."

"I don't give a damn about that. Do you think you can be both father and mother? You're working yourself to the bone, neglecting the kids and you're not making a dime with the marina or the restaurant. I've got money. You can go back to school, finish your degree, go into your own field."

"You are as cold and inhuman as that muscled freak you play. I'm not something you can buy and sell or bribe. You don't give a damn about the kids or me going into my field."

"I don't blame you for feeling that way right now. I tricked you. Maybe I was wrong to do it, but the other night when you were in my arms, I know you felt something for me."

"That was before I knew who you really were."

"I am still the same man. Your response to me was real. We'll find that again, and it will grow—if you'll let it."

Dallas was trembling with fury and with pure raw pain. "I don't want you—ever again."

Without warning, he moved toward her. When she tried to make a run for the door, he barred her way. "There's no escape," he said with a gentleness that belied the terrible power of his will. He caught her chin with the edge of his large hand and forced her to look at him. When she did, she froze. He knew his eyes were blazing with the full, unleashed force of his determination to have her. "Either you marry me, or I'll fight you every step of the way. The press won't leave you alone as soon as they find out you've got my child."

She sucked in her breath and stepped away from him. "Why do they have to find out?"

"Believe me, they will."

"Because you'll tell them?"

"Maybe this once the jackals will be useful to me."

"You are a devil."

He shrugged. "No. but I'd make a bargain with him to get you and the children. Desperate men do desperate things, Dallas. Maybe I don't deserve your trust right now, but the truth is that I want to marry you because I care about you."

"No. This is the easiest way you can think of to get Stephie."

"I want you, too." His voice softened for a moment as he caught her face again in his rough hands. "How can you doubt that? How can you forget how it was when we made love?" As he brushed his knuckles lightly across her cheek, she shivered at the wanton memories, and the sudden heat in her eyes sent flames through him. "Do you really want to live without what we can have together?"

"No!" She bit her lip. "I—I mean yes! I won't think about that night. And I can't stand it when you touch me."

"Can't you?" Christopher's unwavering gaze held hers. Just for an instant he thought he saw love and longing there before her guilt and fury obliterated them.

"The fight will tear Stephie apart," he promised grimly. "Custody fights always hurt the children. I've got money and power and the natural rights of a biological father on my side. What do you have on yours other than the most stubborn nature God ever gave a woamn?"

Dallas tightened her hands into small fists at her sides. "Only the fierce desire to protect Stephie."

"Why can't you see that we want the same thing?"

Dallas turned to flee.

"You have to marry me, Dallas. There's no other way."

Thirteen

The Tiger had won. Today was their wedding day.

In hushed whispers, Stephie and the twins were admiring the beaded silk gown and veil on the bed.

"It looks like the princess's dress!"

It looked like a shroud. Dallas felt numb, unreal, displaced. Nothing in this exquisite bedroom seemed to belong to her. She lifted the cold silk from the bed; downstairs she heard the wedding guests' laughter and gaiety.

She was Christopher's prize. He had terrorized her into this. Today he was triumphant. His beautiful white ranch house was packed with his glamorous friends, his flowers, his champagne and his wedding gifts. Succulent odors from his kitchen where caterers worked drifted up the stairs. Outside on his lawns, blue-and-white tents and picnic tables had been set up. Canopies fluttered over walkways and drives. And beyond were the hills and the Pacific. This was *his* world.

Christopher had given Dallas an upstairs bedroom to change in, and as she slipped into the lavish white gown, she glanced into the mirror and saw that her skin was as white as snow. Stephie and the twins wore matching pink organza dresses, and they were flushed with happiness. When Dallas finished dressing, they began to jump up and down. They had been overjoyed ever since she'd agreed to marry Christopher.

Stephie had said, "I'll have a real family again."

Dallas felt close to tears. What would happen when Stephie's little-girl dream did not come true? What would happen when the marriage inevitably ended, and Stephie lost her brother and sisters and Dallas forever? Dallas knew that if that happened, she would never forgive herself for not fighting Christopher harder.

Still, did she have a choice? As Christopher had predicted, reporters had stormed to the marina and pestered them with endless questions. Suggestive stories that speculated about Dallas's relationship with Christopher had appeared in all the national scandal sheets. When Patrick read one of these stories entitled "*The Tiger*'s Secret Baby" and asked her about it, she had telephoned Christopher begging him to call off his jackals.

"Only you can stop them," he had replied coldly.

"How?"

"By marrying me."

When she had met with her lawyer, who told her that Christopher had very legitimate paternal claims to Stephie, and a legal battle could prove long and expensive, Dallas had grown more terrified. Without money how could she fight him? Then she received a threatening letter from his lawyer. She read it over and over until its message had burned itself into her brain. Another article appeared saying that she had no right to Stephie, that she could offer Stephie none of the advantages Christopher could, that any judge would see that.

Patrick and the twins kept asking why she didn't marry Christopher. They were as afraid of losing Stephie as she was. At last she decided that she couldn't fight them all.

Dallas had called Christopher and agreed to his terms. He'd sent a jet the next morning to pick them up. When she got off the plane, Christopher was at the airport, more handsome than ever now that his hair was its natural reddish gold. His dazzling blue eyes had filled her with warmth. Then she'd seen the press behind him, snapping pictures, screaming questions, and she turned away from him coldly.

His face had grown as closed and distant as hers. Of course, he'd charmed the children because that suited his purpose. But to her, he'd remained cool.

Although they lived together at his ranch house, their relationship hadn't improved. They spoke only when necessary. Often when she was alone she wanted to cry because it all seemed so hopeless, but she was frozen inside. She tried to stall him, but because of Christopher's imminent departure for Spain, he'd insisted they marry at once.

She might have fought longer had not another article appeared: "*The Tiger* Living With Woman Who Has His Secret Baby."

Cal made all the wedding arrangements.

So it was with a troubled heart that Dallas pinned on her wedding veil. She wasn't a real bride. This wasn't her wedding day; this was her funeral.

Robert, who had come to California to give her away, rushed into her bedroom and smiled ecstatically. "Who would have thought you'd do something this sensible?"

Her fingers itched to strangle him. Instead, she threw her bouquet at him, but the flowers bounced off his chest.

"Why can't you act like a normal brother and console me?"

"That's normal?" He looked at his watch. He stooped to pick up the tangle of blossoms and streamers. "Girls, y'all run along downstairs."

When they were alone, Dallas said, "I—I can't go through with it."

"Nonsense." He replaced her bouquet into her shaking hands. "All you have is bridal jitters."

"You only want this because you're such a social climber!"

"Hell. Who else would marry you? You've got four kids, a money-losing marina, a couple of worthless English degrees, no money, impractical expectations..."

"While you're listing my assets, don't forget to mention a supportive big brother."

"This is the real world."

"You're telling me."

"He loves you."

"No. He's had all those other women. Starlets..."

"So what? You have a past."

She turned as white as her dress. "It's not the same."

"Oh, because you're a woman, you get to play by different rules?"

"Of all the low-down, sexist—"

"Look, he was a bachelor, in grief over his little girl. He was rich, famous. Most of those women threw themselves at him. One of them broke into his house. He found her naked in his bed when he came home one night. He was drunk. She was beautiful. He was lonely. He wanted her. But he threw her out. She went to the press and said he'd brought her there and tried to seduce her. She even sued him for palimony."

"How do you know that?"

"He told me."

"Did he tell you he loves me?"

"He's marrying you, isn't he?"

"That doesn't mean anything!" she cried softly.

"I've seen the way he looks at you. The kids adore him."

"He's only doing this to strengthen his claim to Stephie."

"You're wrong, Dallas."

"Oh, why is it that you've never once listened to me?"

Robert patted her hand. "Can we work on that one later? The wedding march is beginning."

Dallas was so heartsick that she wanted to throw herself down on the bed. Robert was pulling her toward the door. She drew a deep, resigned breath, and she let him lead her down the stairs. But with every trancelike step, her heart knocked madly with unbearable dread.

When they reached the threshold in the immense living room crammed with guests, the air grew thick with the cloying fragrances of a thousand flowers—roses, carnations, orchids, irises. Dallas's hand went to her throat. She was suffocating, dying. Then she saw Christopher standing in a pool of sunlight beside the minister and the children. His cool blue gaze slid to her as if to impel her forward.

She stood frozen where she was.

An expectant hush fell upon the crowd as she pushed Robert away, but she saw only Christopher. His dark features seemed chiseled of stone. If she'd hoped to see some softness in him, she found none.

Never had he seemed grimmer. He didn't want her. He was using her to get his child as he had used other women— to forget his grief. He was a movie star, and she knew nothing about him except what she'd read. He wasn't real. She was an ordinary woman who couldn't mean anything to him. Dallas closed her eyes because she couldn't look at him without loving him.

No. She couldn't still love him. She had loved a dream. This man was an indomitable stranger, and the thought of marrying him chilled her.

"No—"

Her soft cry rang out above the dying strains of the wedding march. All eyes were upon her—some politely curious, some covertly hostile. She felt only Christopher's.

For an instant she didn't realize she'd spoken.

Then she knew that no matter what he did to her, she couldn't marry him. Not if he didn't love her. Maybe she would lose Stephie anyway, but she had to fight for her. And even as she knew this, she was sorry she couldn't marry him. He would never know how sorry.

Alone, she faced Christopher across that throng. In his black tux, he looked menacingly huge. He had the power, the legal rights and the money to crush her for this humiliation.

She turned her back on him and walked out of the house to the waiting limousine that was there to whisk them away to their honeymoon. She heard Christopher's racing footsteps behind her.

She was opening the white car door when he caught her. His hand closed over her wrist, and she winced as he pinned her against the car.

"I can't, Christopher," she whispered. "I tried, but I can't."

She expected violence.

He drew a ragged breath and stepped back. "You've always been afraid of me," he said quietly.

"I was right to be." She searched the grim darkness of his bleak face and felt fresh despair because she could read no softness for her there. The blue eyes were hard. His mouth was set. She couldn't tell him that she had been afraid of loving him, that she was still afraid of it any more than she could tell him that she loved him anyway.

"You can go," he said at last, bringing her hand to his warm lips and kissing her fingers.

"What?"

"I won't have you afraid of me."

The children were huddled together on the veranda, and she called to them.

They stayed where they were, not wanting to come.

"It's okay, guys," Christopher said. "The fight's over. You've got to go home with your aunt."

When they came slowly forward, Christopher knelt down and looked into Stephie's eyes. "I won't fight you for Stephie," he said to Dallas. "You're right. She belongs with all of you."

Stephie's big dark eyes grew luminous as she studied her father. Then she threw her arms around him and clung. So did Patrick. Both children began to sniffle quietly. The twins stared at Dallas, their pretty identical faces tragic.

"Some day you'll all understand," Dallas said.

"You'll probably marry someone dumb like Gordon," the twins said.

"Girls, it's over." Christopher's voice was clipped and final. "You have to go home with your aunt."

"We want to stay."

"I'll be on location in Spain."

"Will we ever see you again?" Patrick asked.

"Hell." Christopher ruffled Patrick's yellow hair that was so like his own. "That's hard to say."

"Maybe . . . someday?"

"Right. Someday."

Had Christopher looked at Dallas he would have seen the single glistening tear that traced down her white cheek. But he was looking at the children.

Dallas brushed the tear away and got into the limousine. She sank back against plush white leather, thankful for the sound of the air conditioner drowning out the children's goodbyes. In the short time they had known him, all of them had come to love him.

At last they were in the car. Christopher leaned down to the window and said to Patrick, "Don't go out on that sailboard alone, and don't leave your skateboard on those stairs anymore, either." To Dallas he said, "I'll have your things sent."

"There's no hurry."

Although Christopher looked away at the Pacific, as if he couldn't bear to look at her, she couldn't tear her gaze away from him. His eyes were the same dazzling blue as the ocean's. Pain constricted in her chest. She would never see him again.

"The offer's open," he muttered in that strange indifferent voice he'd used ever since she'd come to California. "If you change your mind, call Cal. He'll put you in touch."

Look at me! All you have to do is tell me you love me!

He straightened his long lean body and backed away.

She felt desolate.

The limousine was driving away; everyone but Dallas turned around to wave goodbye. Clouds of dust swirled behind the limousine.

Patrick said in a low dismal voice, "I can't see him anymore."

Everyone turned around and grew still and silent. Dallas could feel them blaming her.

When the limo jolted over the cattle guard and out the gate, Stephie tugged at Dallas's sleeve. "Why wouldn't you marry my daddy?"

"I—I..."

Stephie's eyes were so dark and imploring that Dallas couldn't answer her. Instead she looked out the window.

Magnificent headlands jutted out into a beautiful blue ocean. This beautiful, warmly sparkling day was to have been her wedding day. Tonight would have been her wedding night.

She had fought to escape that fate and had won.

Why, then, did her victory feel so hollow?

Why was the pain in her heart so intense that she wanted to die?

Fourteen

Life went on at the marina, but not as before. Dallas and the children seemed to have regressed back to that awful time after Carrie and Nick had died. Only this period was darker, blacker—more profound. This was new grief piled onto old.

Stephie cried at night and had to be constantly watched because she walked in her sleep. Dallas's nightmares were more frequent. She would wake up and long for Christopher's comforting arms about her before she reminded herself of his treachery. The twins took up with their wild crowd again, and every day they became more difficult to handle. Oscar felt the tension and drank more. So Dallas worked harder, and accomplished less. Robert told her that the kids' insurance money was almost gone.

Christopher had left his yacht at the marine; Oscar was supposed to take care of it. But when he drank, he forgot to check the bilge pump and the lines. So Dallas found herself doing these things. Every time that she stepped into Christopher's cabin to pump the bilge, she remembered the happy times and the sad times she'd spent with him there. Funny, as the days passed, how hard it became to recall the bad times. Funny, how it got harder to hate him and easier to love him.

At first she had been too ashamed to allow herself to dwell on their night of passion. But gradually her anger dissolved, and her softer, truer feelings emerged. She remembered the lean glory of his naked body writhing on top of hers. She remembered the hot force of his mouth burning gently across her skin. But most of all she remembered his tendernesses, his kindnesses. If he were so bad, why had he helped her with the kids, with the restaurant, with her acceptance of herself?

She lay awake in her bed and tortured herself by imagining him there, his calloused hands exploring her until she quivered, imagining his hot lips tracing over her body. She drove herself mad, remembering him.

He never called or wrote.

And every day that he didn't, the ache to have him near, to hear his voice, to feel his touch grew inside her.

Was he forgetting her?

The days dragged by, suffocatingly hot, scorching days.

Rennie found a picture of Christopher's beautiful costar in a magazine that Dallas took and shredded into a hundred pieces. But she couldn't forget the girl's bewitching green eyes, or the seductive promise of her pouting lips.

One night at supper, during a lull in the conversation, Patrick said, "I wonder if he misses us, too?"

No one had to ask who he was.

"Of course," Stephie said wisely, piercing a pea with her fork and bringing it to the tip of her nose so she could inspect it with her crossed eyes.

"He hasn't written or called," Patrick said, echoing Dallas's silent worries. "It's been a month."

"I know how long it's been," Dallas snapped. "Of course he's forgotten us."

The twins rushed to his defense. "Maybe he's just hurt."

"His name is Stone isn't it?" Dallas said. "That's what he's made of."

The look that passed between all four kids infuriated Dallas. "You're going to ruin your eyes if you don't quit staring at that pea, Stephie. Either put it down or eat it!"

"I don't like peas." Stephie set her fork down defiantly.

"It's rude to say insulting things about food, young lady."

"It's rude of you to say mean things about my daddy. Why do you hate him?"

Dallas was stung to the quick. "I—I don't hate him."

No one was pretending to eat anymore. They were all looking accusingly at Dallas until she felt very uncomfortable.

"Look, surely you don't still think I'm the bad guy, do you?"

"Oh, no, Aunt Dallas." They shook their heads.

"Then why don't we all get back to eating our dinners?"

Not a single fork lifted.

The next day, Christopher's telephone calls began. He always asked for the children, never for Dallas. They would talk to him by the hour, and she would feel absurdly left out. And every night when he called, the ache for him inside her grew.

She loved her children, but she needed another adult to share her thoughts and little every-day crises. She had grown used to leaning on Christopher, to counting on his help and advice and comfort. Who was she kidding? She wanted him. She loved him. She couldn't forget him.

And never did she want him more than the morning that the letter from the adoption agency came. When she read the name on the envelope of the agency she'd given her baby to, she didn't dare open it until Christopher called that night.

Only when she heard the phone ring and Patrick shout his name did she slit the envelope. Inside, was a letter from the adoptive parents of her baby. It told of their gratitude to her for the gift of their beautiful daughter; it told how they loved her more than anything.

Blue ink blurred through Dallas's tears of joy as she read of her daughter's successes. Like her mother, her daughter was number one in her school class.

Dallas clasped the letter to her heart. Her little girl wrote poetry and was going to major in English. She was a highbrow. *Like her mother.*

A picture and a poem that Dallas hadn't noticed fell from the envelope. She picked them up and studied the photograph. Her little girl was a beautiful young woman. The poem was a letter of love to her birth mother.

Dallas's hand began to shake as she looked at the phone on the bedside table. Christopher was talking to the children. More than anything she wanted to share her wonderful news with him. But her fingers froze when she touched the receiver.

He didn't love her. All he had ever wanted from her was his child.

When Patrick stepped into the bedroom a few minutes later, he found his aunt in tears. When she saw him, she yanked her hand from the phone so he wouldn't see.

But he saw. "You want to talk to him, don't you?"

She shook her head.

"Pick it up," he said gently.

"I—I can't."

Patrick strode slowly into the room like a little man. Very methodically he lifted the phone. "Aunt Dallas is in bed crying because she misses you and wants you to come back!"

Dallas grabbed the phone. "That's not true! I was crying because I got a letter from the adoption agency about my baby."

"Kids, hang up!"

The downstairs extension clicked.

"Was it good news or bad?" Christopher asked quietly.

She could feel the tension in him, his genuine concern. She was only talking to him on the telephone, but she felt connected to him—body and soul.

She held her breath. Now. She should hang up on him.

Why did she cling to the receiver as if it were a lifeline? "Good..." she whispered at last.

Across thousands of miles of ocean, she felt his joy at her happiness in the warm timbre of his voice. "Honey, that's wonderful."

She was filled with a golden happiness.

For a second longer she held on to the receiver.

"Dallas, I—"

More than anything she wanted to hear what he was going to say. But she hung up.

Only to be instantly sorry.

The next day was a nightmare. Dallas had heard from her child, and she had spoken to the man she loved. In a single hour she had made contact with two of the people she had loved and lost. She had felt Christopher's joy for her, his intense caring. Then she had willfully, stupidly ruined everything.

If he had deceived her, she had been equally cruel. She began to think that she had been blind to him, that she had judged him unfairly before she had even known him.

If only he would call again, she would tell him how sorry she was for everything.

But he didn't call.

If the children were very disappointed, she was crushed, and she knew it was her fault.

She had lost him—again.

All day she tormented herself by thoughts of him turning to his costar for solace. As the day ended, her longing for him grew.

It was a beautiful warm summer night, and the moon was nearly full. After she put the children to bed, she was too miserable to sleep. So she stepped out for a solitary walk along the beach. As she wandered toward the causeway bridge she saw a strange apparition.

The knight from Stephie's fairy tale was riding toward Dallas on a white horse and leading another behind him. The moonlight gilded the knight's bright hair. The breeze blew it across his brow. He shook his head faintly.

She knew that gesture.

Christopher.

But he was in Spain. She had lost him forever.

The ghostly knight came nearer. Her heart seemed to stop beating.

It was Christopher in a suit of dull tarnished mail.

She froze. Then she was running toward him, her gauzy skirt flying, her golden hair loose and spreading about her shoulders. She stopped breathlessly just before she reached him.

They devoured one another with their eyes.

"I'm sorry," she said on a low whisper.

The horses whinnied softly.

"So am I."

"I love you," she said. "I love you."

"I know."

"You do? How could—"

He leaned over and tried to lift her onto his horse, but his armor made it hard for him to move. "Put your foot in the stirrup," he commanded.

She did, and he pulled her up.

"Your armor's all black."

"It was the best Wardrobe could manage-on such short notice. I imagined you'd think it suited me better than the shining stuff."

"It's cold, too."

"Stop complaining. You should be wearing it."

"Why did you come back?"

He took a quick breath. "Don't you know?"

She felt his golden hair brush against her forehead as he pulled her against his armor and kissed her. His lips were hot and wild, and she felt the pent-up agony of all the fierce hunger in him that had brought him back to her. The hand at her neck held her close while his other arm crushed her against his armored chest. Dallas clung to him; she was as shaken as he. His mouth moved roughly across her face to her throat.

"Honey, I couldn't stay away. God help me, I tried. I tried to forget you, to blot out all the memories."

"So did I."

"But the harder I tried, the stronger they got."

"You're a movie star."

"Until you came into my life, that fate was a sentence in hell."

"You really want me? And not just because of Stephie?"

"Oh, Dallas..." He broke off in a sigh. "There has never been any woman I've wanted more." He caught her face in his hands, holding it still. "Aren't you going to make me say it?"

"What?"

He grinned. "You know."

"What?"

"That I love you, you little idiot. I love you. Only you."

"You said you didn't know much about love."

"I didn't—until I met a good teacher. You taught me everything I ever needed to know."

"Where did you get the horses?"

"Cal had them flown in from my ranch. The second one is for Stephie."

"She's in bed now. Do you want to see her?"

"Later. Much later," he whispered. "Now, the only thing I want is you."

She looked into his eyes and saw his love as well as the pain she had caused him. For an instant, she was filled with guilt.

She would spend the rest of her life making it up to him. And she would start tonight.

She arched her body to fit his and her gauzy skirt rode up her thighs.

Christopher closed his eyes and took a deep breath.

Then she reached up and began to kiss him.

They were on his boat, their pulses throbbing as they tore off their clothes. He came to her, and he was so breathtakingly magnificent that she touched him first, her impatient hands moving over him boldly, stirring the hot flames of his passion until he could stand it no longer and clasped her tightly against the hard contours of his body. Her heartbeats accelerated as his mouth claimed hers.

He had come back for her.

Not just for Stephie.

Most of all for her, too.

His large hands closed over her breasts.

He had come back for her—and this glorious knowledge made everything he did for her in bed more wonderful. He began to kiss her—everywhere—until her throat was hot and her skin was ice.

His golden head lowered and his tongue licked sensitive flesh, sending a livid tingling current of desire tracing warmly through her. She moaned softly.

Fire and ice; she had felt them before. But only for him.

"I have to have you," she whispered desperately.

"At last you admit it," he said quietly.

At last.

He drew her down onto the bunk beneath him. Her golden hair spread out beneath his brown arms. His lips burned hers, and then he kissed her eyelids, her cheek, her earlobe, passionately, murmuring love words.

It seemed to her that every inch of her body was covered by the heat of his, and the ice was dissolving in the fire of his passion. For an instant he was very still. His eyes met hers, and she saw all his love as well as fierce need. He brushed her cheek tenderly with a fingertip. A familiar welcoming warmth seemed to flow in the depths of her body. It seemed to her that all her life she had waited for this moment.

"I love you," he whispered. "Only you. There will never be anyone but you."

"I love you, too."

Then he was inside her. And what happened after that was too wonderful for words.

Epilogue

Dallas was a bride in misting white. Again she hesitated on the threshold of Christopher's immense living room crammed with wedding guests. Only because this time, the sight of Christopher standing beside the minister with the children filled her with happiness.

Again the house was filled with flowers and friends. Only this time Dallas's golden-haired birth child and her adoptive parents were there. Marguerite had come, as well.

Outside, the sun was shining and the Pacific was sparkling. Tents and canopies had been set up. The white horses were wearing garlands of flowers. It all seemed like a wonderful dream. Dallas felt that she was a princess, and that Christopher's white house was as dazzling as the white castle in Stephie's story. And Christopher had turned out to be her knight after all.

Dallas caught the rhythm of the wedding march, and a white satin toe peeped out from beneath her skirt. Hesitating no longer, she took the first step. Surely this was the happiest moment of her life.

When she reached the alter, Christopher held out his hand, and as she reached for it and let him pull her close, she knew that at last she had found love.

Here by his side was where she had belonged, where she would always belong.

They were a couple. Part of a family.

They would love each other forever.

* * * * *

NORA ROBERTS

Love has a language all its own, and for centuries,
flowers have symbolized love's finest expression.
Discover the language of flowers—and love—in
this romantic collection of 48 favorite books by
bestselling author Nora Roberts.

Starting in February 1992, two titles will be
available each month at your favorite retail outlet.

In February, look for:

Irish Thoroughbred, Volume #1
The Law Is A Lady, Volume #2

Collect all 48 titles and become fluent in the
Language of Love.

LOL192

THE LANGUAGE of LOVE

Silhouette Special Edition

salutes

MOMENTS OF GLORY

from Lindsay McKenna

In a country torn with conflict, in a time of bitter passions, these brave men and women wage a war against all odds... and a timeless battle for honor, for fleeting moments of glory, for the promise of enduring love.

February: RIDE THE TIGER (#721) Survivor Dany Villard is wise to the love-'em-and-leave-'em ways of war, but wounded hero Gib Ramsey swears she's captured his heart... forever.

March: ONE MAN'S WAR (#727) The war raging inside brash and bold Captain Pete Mallory threatens to destroy him, until Tess Ramsey's tender love guides him toward peace.

April: OFF LIMITS (#733) Soft-spoken Marine Jim McKenzie saved Alexandra Vance's life in Vietnam; now he needs her love to save his honor....

Silhouette Romance®

LONG, TALL TEXANS

DONAVAN
Diana Palmer

Diana Palmer's bestselling LONG, TALL TEXANS series continues with DONAVAN....

From the moment elegant Fay York walked into the bar on the wrong side of town, rugged Texan Donavan Langley knew she was trouble. But the lovely young innocent awoke a tenderness in him that he'd never known...and a desire to make her a proposal she couldn't refuse....

Don't miss DONAVAN by Diana Palmer, the ninth book in her LONG, TALL TEXANS series. Coming in January...only from Silhouette Romance.

LTT192

YOU'VE ASKED FOR IT, YOU'VE GOT IT!

MAN OF THE MONTH: 1992

ONLY FROM

SILHOUETTE® Desire™

You just couldn't get enough of them, those sexy men from Silhouette Desire—twelve sinfully sexy, delightfully devilish heroes. Some will make you sweat, some will make you sigh...but every long, lean one of them will have you swooning. So here they are, men we couldn't resist bringing to you for one more year....

A KNIGHT IN TARNISHED ARMOR
by Ann Major in January

THE BLACK SHEEP
by Laura Leone in February

THE CASE OF THE MESMERIZING BOSS
by Diana Palmer in March

DREAM MENDER
by Sheryl Woods in April

WHERE THERE IS LOVE
by Annette Broadrick in May

BEST MAN FOR THE JOB
by Dixie Browning in June

Don't let these men get away! *Man of the Month*, only in Silhouette Desire.